Clocks Locks Corpses!

And Other Epic Horror Poems

S. Jayne Bradley

ROOKERY

Book Cover by Rachel McPhee

Cover Fonts are copywritten by https://www.freepik.com/font/gilligan-shutteran d and https://www.1001fonts.com/zombie-holocaust-font.html

Illustrations by https://pixabay.com/users/aeltev-2799234/

1st edition 2024

978-1-7386183-5-4 Clocks Locks Corpses (New Zealand Paperback)
978-1-7386183-6-1 Clocks Locks Corpses (Kindle)
978-1-7386183-7-8 Clocks Locks Corpses (Ebook)
978-1-7386183-8-5 Clocks Locks Corpses (Print-on-Demand via Draft2Digital)
978-1-7386183-9-2 Clocks Locks Corpses (Amazon Print-on-Demand)

Horse And Norm originally printed in North Shore Writers Group Anthology - 2023: Fire on Water 978-1-7386183-3-0. Reprinted here with all permissions.

Table of Contents

S. Jayne Bradley

Clocks Locks Corpses

The first thing is first, so where do I start?
I suppose we'll begin with a young London tart,
Upon a dark street awaiting a date,
Knowing full well it was getting late

The lamps that were burning provided some light
But it wasn't enough to keep out the night
The fog rolled in thick, and the air had turned cold
It was not a night for the sick or the old

But stand there she did in her blue velvet dress
Not knowing her organs would soon be a mess
That her long golden hair would be covered in blood
Or that her blue dress would be splattered with mud

In silence she waited alone on the street
Shaking her shoulders and tapping her feet
With hopes that a man would take her away
To a place that was warm for a quick easy lay

And deep in the darkness a horror drew near
That would make a grown man quiver with fear
Hard snapping jaws and teeth now stained brown
Was lurking down alleys in old London Town

Clocks Locks Corpses!

As she stood waiting a shadow appeared
With a wide lurid smile and dark eyes that leered
With cold rotting hands it groped at her neck
Turning her into a shivering wreck.

Then of her flesh its teeth took a bite
Her cry of pure pain had shattered the night
But soon they both wore identical grins
And this is the place where the story begins

In March of eighteen thirty-two
Experiments beneath a zoo
Released a nasty kind of flu
That makes folk want to feast on you

A few miles east from where the tart stood
In a quiet old house in a rough neighbourhood
Our hero, a man, had sat deep in thought
Beside a roast dinner a servant had brought

The house was not large and mostly of brick
The windows were wide, and the walls were quite thick
His fortune was small but enough to get by
He often made money without having to try

No more than eighteen and out on his own
Too young some had said to be all alone
But our hero was clever, more clever than most
Though not smart enough to cook his own roast

He was born of good blood not quite noble birth
The boy had left home to seek his own worth
His father worked steel, his mother a maid
And his fate would be service, that is if he stayed

So, our hero had left to find his own place,
Where no one would know of his past or his face
And things had been fine, at least for a while
He lived it up grand, he lived life in style

Blue were his eyes, and dark was his hair,
He had a fine smile but to see it was rare,
He always dressed well and kept with the time
His posture, his manner was truly sublime

All of his charm would not make him prepared
For something that would, like the others run scared
A plague of undead would rise from the grave
And teach our young hero what it means to be brave

In March of eighteen thirty-two
He said farewell to all he knew
The living died and numbers grew
Of folk that want to chew on you

Our hero had sat with things on his mind
Scribbling notes on what scraps he could find
Something was wrong he thought in his head
As he sipped on his tea and chewed on his bread

He wondered how long it'd been since he'd slept
'Cause into his dreams bad things had now crept
He walked to the window and stared at the road
What did this darkness and thick fog forbode?

In the distance he heard a cry in the night
Then followed by a call of delight
His hair stood on end and his skin had turned pale
He soon brushed it off as the howl of a gale

Clocks Locks Corpses!

And something deep down had nagged and complained
That what he had heard could not be explained
The grandfather clock had chimed in at three
And he knew that his bed was the best place to be

A strange sense of need made him lock up his door
It was a strong feeling he couldn't ignore,
He bolted his room, the curtains were drawn
He climbed into bed and awaited the dawn

When his eyes closed, and he rested his head
He had no idea that people were dead
That they were moving around feeding on flesh
Or that it was best when screaming and fresh

If his dreams had been nightmares he would never know
Though his night passed quick, outside it passed slow
And when he'd awake his life would be new
A new life of blood, of death and of spew

In March of eighteen thirty-two
The folk want to feast on you
The hunt begins, their prey is you
There is no hope you'll make it through

When the sun had returned so mockingly bright
Our hero awoke to a bone chilling sight
There were hand prints of blood on all window panes
And on all the ledges sat, bones, and brains

He scrambled from bed; heart raced in his chest
And fumbled with buttons on a smart winter vest
He pulled on his pants and his watch and chain
His hundreds of questions ensnaring his brain

When he opened the door, he gave a loud yelp
At what remained of his own hired help
Their bodies in pieces, our hero aggrieved
They did not deserve the fate they received

"Perhaps 'twas a robber," he said with a frown
And hoped there was help in old London Town
But to find folk in pieces around his nice flat
And thought that no human could ever do that

He decided to leave, he'd not stick around
And then he had heard a blood curdling sound
Someone else was invading his space
Someone who left his own bloody trace

Curiosity came so he drew ever near
Until it became revoltingly clear
When his eyes fell upon the horrible sight
His stomach was churning as he smelled this blight

It looked like a man, but it glared with black eyes
It was crouched on the floor then it started to rise
Clutched in one hand was a broken leg bone
It caught sight of our hero and started to moan

In March of eighteen thirty-two
A side of life he never knew
A world of death of blood and spew
An image of a world askew

Seeing the danger, he found himself in
Shining from jaws and Cheshire grin
Our hero then turned and ran for his life
Stopping just once for his pistol and knife

He heard the thing coming up close from behind
And he felt his own sanity begin to unwind
He turned by the stairs facing off with his foe
As he lifted his gun, time started to slow

With a fiery bang and a puff of black smoke
The smell of it made him splutter and choke
And fresh crimson blood was sprayed on the wall
But the creature before him did not even fall

Half of its head now lay on the ground
And from its blue lips came a gurgling sound
Without much more thought around he had spun
And down the wide stairs, he started to run

He pushed the door open and through it he ran
Behind him came running the thing, not a man,
And the ice in the wind and over the stones
Had bothered him less than the blood and the bones

In unending silence, the streets had remained
He glanced back behind, saw the creature had gained
Then something happened he did not expect
More creatures appeared in droves left unchecked

They came from the alleys and the wide-open doors
Covered in knife wounds, boils, and sores
They all seemed to wear the same jagged tooth grin
And our hero, he knew, alone he'd not win

In March of eighteen thirty-two
There isn't much that you can do,
Find some friends who are true blue
To fight off those who'll feast on you

They moaned and howled like beasts left unfed
Their eyes showed no life like the long-buried dead
The smell in the air was a thick stench of death
Though he was fast he was soon out of breath

He pushed himself on, but he started to ache
Perhaps choosing to run had been a mistake
The wind started blowing and the air turned much colder
And he felt a warm hand grab a hold of his shoulder

The last thing he heard was his pocket watch tick
It swirled in his head, the feeling would stick
The screeching grew faint, and he fell to the ground
And suddenly soothed by a loud ticking sound

He awoke with a start in a cold quiet place
And wiped all the sweat from his neck and his face
He then sat up straight and looked all around
To examine the place in which he'd been found

It was damp and quite dark with only one light
The walls were of brick and were painted white
There was only one door that was made of thick steel
It had a thin slot and a red rubber seal

The door it then opened, and he leapt to his feet
Not sure of the person that he would now meet
Of all of the people he thought would be there
He did not expect a girl with red hair

Her dark eyes had smiled behind wire frames
And beckoned him on without asking for names
He followed her out into the next room
Leaving the darkness, the gloom, and the doom,

His eyes looked around the passage they walked
And she made him hush up each time that he talked
But he didn't mind; he liked her sweet smile
He could handle the quiet, if for only a while

In March of eighteen thirty-two
When your friends are numbered few
A group, a bunch, a band, a crew
Will find a way of helping you

The room they had entered was filled with bright light,
He shielded his eyes to regain his sight
Then he could see he was in a lab
He saw to his left a giant stone slab

There were bottles and liquids and tiny glass vials
And the entire room was wall to wall tiles
There was a loud ticking that echoed his heart
And then a voice said, "Now where shall I start?"

"You could tell me why I am here in this place,
And tell me what happened to the human race.
Why are they hungry for blood and for skin?
How did this horrible story begin?"

He turned to the voice who had started to speak
And looked on in shock and thought *What a freak*
For who stood before him appeared to be frail
His one working eye, was milky and pale

The man had one arm and was missing his legs
Which had been replaced with mechanical pegs
What was once a left hand was now a brass claw
The fact he breathed still filled our hero with awe

"I am a doctor," The man said with such pride
"You've joined a few others in the best place to hide
For the streets are now crawling with the hungry undead
Who will eat all your organs and feast on your head

"You are lucky we found you," the red-haired girl said
"If left any longer you would have been dead."
"Thanks for your kindness," our hero replied
Claxons then sounded, he looked on wide eyed.

In March of Eighteen thirty-two
Explanations now overdue
But there is nothing you can do
Unless the one in charge is you

"I found one outside," a beefy man called
Our hero looked in feeling shocked and appalled
"This one's got fight, thank God for the chains.
If I'd let him get closer he'd have gotten my brains."

The three of them pulled it into the room
Our hero then smelled the thick stench of doom
As they forced it down onto the stone slab
With a long needle the doc gave a jab

When the chains were secure they took a step back
Expecting the creature to try and attack
It glared with dark eyes and struggled in vain
And showed the desire to cause them all pain

"What are you doing?" our hero cried out
"Please tell me now what this is about."
The girl with red hair she turned to the doc
"It's all about ticking and that giant clock."

"You see what we've found is though they are dead
They still can be filled with fear and with dread
The great ticking clock, it beats like a heart
It reminds them of things of which they're a part

And don't you dare judge, we're finding a cure
Despite all our actions, our intentions are pure
You're lucky we need your help here at all
We could have just left you when we heard your call."

"I'm sorry, I'm sorry," our hero replied
Feeling like he was on some kind of ride
He watched them intently, the work had begun
Confused and afraid of what they had done

In March of eighteen thirty-two
The doctor has a plan he drew
To find a cure, a new breakthrough
For those who want to chew on you

"I know you have questions," the doctor then said
He glanced at our hero with a twitch of his head
"You cannot defeat them with sheer force alone
It will take us much more than a lock and a stone."

Our hero examined the doctor's good eye
He shook his head sadly and heaved a great sigh
He could see they were helping but something felt wrong
The doctor's great plan might fail before long

The doctor then grinned with his old broken teeth
The ticking got stronger, it thrummed from beneath
But if it had mattered, they did not explain
They all seemed to have other things on the brain

"Let me show you my plan and all of my schemes
You'd never believe not even in dreams
You'll understand why the beating heart beats
And why those poor people crave fresh human meats."

Our hero looked down and straightened his vest
Feeling that now he was in for a test
Not of his bones but the strength of his mind
For he was unsure what horrors he'd find

The doctor then grabbed him and led him away
As they walked through the doors, he started to pray
The light it had grown, and burned like bright fire
And he was in darkness to what would transpire

Apprehensive our hero had followed the doc
Preparing himself for some kind of shock
They walked down the hall to a rather large door
Where blood had been splattered all over the floor

In March of eighteen thirty-two
There are some things that are not true
Broken tools now shined up new
The one who sees it is not you

"Now don't be afraid, of what is inside
There's many a secret, in you I'll confide
Promise me this, now you're part of my team,
When I open the door, please try not to scream,"

The door opened slowly, and he closed his blue eyes
He was not at all ready for this sick surprise
The doctor then shunted him in a dark room
The thick humid air it reeked like a tomb

There was a faint moaning like a scraping of stone
Now greatly afraid of what he'd be shown
When he opened his eyes two more then leered back
And he saw the mouth grinning even in the deep black

"I know you are frightened," The doctor then said
"But they're all behind bars, my pets the undead
I've tried ways to cure them, but alas no avail
And their spawning is also a horrible tale."

The room had been built like a prison or jail
With no ventilation the air had grown stale
 Broken dead bodies would beat at the bars
Covered with wounds, dead flesh, and old scars

The knocking and scraping made our hero feel sick
He knew he had to get out of there quick
But the doctor would not let go of his arm
Giving our hero great cause for alarm

In March of eighteen thirty-two
These are the things I know to be true
The day a scientist would rue
By spawning the folk who'll feast on you

"A few months ago, in the deepest of cold
The winter had come as I had been told
In secret a scientist went down below
Under a zoo that was closed due to snow

Under the cages in a place now disused
A scientist worked and books he perused
And studied the things that some wouldn't dare
But he wanted the glory, and he did not care

His thoughts bent on making a new kind of cure
But what he'd been curing no-one could be sure
It started with rats and moved to an ape
Not thinking at all his work would escape

At last, his great effort for man, it was ready,
He had poured in his soul, his feet now unsteady
The results came out wrong and the man passed away
But somehow his body had wanted to stay

The scientist's mind was growing quite lame
Perhaps his weak memory was what he could blame
One cage left unlocked, and a door left ajar
Who knew that this sickness could travel so far?

Down a small passage and into fresh air
A creature released and a world unaware
And before it escaped on its master it fed
And out in the world its illness would spread

Shuffling and stumbling through deep drifts of snow,
To a city awake with an unearthly glow
It only knew darkness and the light was so fresh,
And its hunger had grown for warm human flesh."

In March of eighteen thirty-two
The scientist's work they must undo
But from our hero's point of view
There was not much that he could do

Our hero had listened to the story so well
The doctors calm voice had him under a spell
"Now that you know the story my friend,
I hope you will stay and help with its end."

The doctor then led him out of the gloom
And into the light of another tiled room
In the middle a table where four others sat
As well as a large, morose ginger cat

"Please now be seated and enjoy our fine meal,
As fine as we get since we have to steal."
Our hero sat down and bowed his young head
And he said his own prayer before breaking his bread

"Now how does a boy of no more than eighteen,
Survive the rough streets and come out so clean?
There's not a scratch on him," a beefy man said
"By all my accounts, this boy should be dead"

Our hero looked up, stopped eating his meal
Not knowing at all of how he should feel
He swallowed his food and gave it some thought
Then tried to explain how he'd not gotten caught

He eyed up their faces and remembered that day
The thing in his house and how he'd got away
"Some say that I'm fast, that I'm quick on my feet.
And I can outrun every soul that I meet,"

They all exchanged glances and the beefy man smiled
"It's good to see folk, even though you're a child,"
Our hero just laughed and continued to feed
Staying felt right, a good thing indeed

In March of eighteen thirty-two
Joy had come but death was due
An end to this was not in view
Their eyes saw things they never knew.

A few weeks had passed, and our hero fit in
None could resist his wide charming grin
And where pain had endured, he'd started to care
As our hero found love with the girl with red hair

To cover his feelings of loss and despair,
To be so alone, he'd pretend he could bare
And to find someone else, who had faced the same,
Became in this darkness, a bright shining flame

At first, he'd just smile, and then make her tea
Her heart was a lock and he'd find a key
With fiery hair and ice in her eyes
Them falling in love could mean their demise

She'd shaken him off, the first hundred tries
But she had been fighting, her own butterflies
She had to tell him her long-standing fear
That she could then lose him if he'd gotten near

Their lips had then met like fingers and hands
He touched her red hair and played with the strands
No more would their journey be endured all alone
Now that together their hearts had been sewn

Afraid that their love would cause others great pain
They kept it a secret although 'twas in vain
For the walls they have eyes and they always see
Even in safety they had never been free

For the doctor had plans the others knew not
They were devices in a devious plot
Now, things were happy but then soon enough
Things would become so horribly tough

In April eighteen thirty-two
Some things occur you can't undo
The loss of limbs replaced anew
A beating heart you can't subdue

Our hero had found that he worked quite well
Out in the streets of the city of hell
With the great beefy man who called himself Rob
Who was good with a knife but a bit of a slob

Their first week in London the streets had been filled
If they hadn't been careful, they could have been killed
The undead were hunting for human remains
Searching for flesh and hungry for brains

When they ventured out the streets had stayed still,
They hardly ran into the things they could kill
This worried them more than anything could
If things got this dull, it meant nothing good

On one fateful day when the rain had been cleared
A horrid event confirmed what they feared
Out all alone in the wide empty city
They came from the shadows, no fear, pain, or pity

Rob heard them coming from far down the street
The screaming of voices and pounding of feet
They exchanged scared glances then started to run
The chase to end chases had quickly begun

It became deafening, a god-awful sound
The stomping of feet it shook through the ground
Our hero and Rob, they ran to escape
Hoping they'd find a way out of this scrape

In April eighteen thirty-two
With a feeling of that Déjà vu
Through the empty streets they flew
Not knowing what they'd run into

Even though he was big, our Rob he was fast
But he didn't know if his body would last
A few steps ahead our hero kept pace
He balanced his breathing, it wasn't a race

Then came the smell of warm rotting meat
The fact they weren't sick was some kind of feat
Their two pounding hearts were keeping the beat
And knowing full well that the creatures would eat

A scraping of stones and a loud heavy thud
Our hero looked back, sounds chilling his blood
Rob, he had slipped and fallen down hard
And our hero ran back though still on his guard

"Come on you great lump," our hero then said
"Get up on your feet, you're not made of lead."
He grabbed at Rob's hand and pulled him along
With the smell and the sound growing ever so strong

Then like a nightmare spawned directly from hell
They saw with their eyes the source of the smell
With eyes black as midnight that shone in the light
It did not stop running and it wanted to bite

Rob jumped to his feet with our hero behind
The creatures now hunting for the flesh they could find
Their skin hung in chunks revealing their bones
Their now toeless feet slapped on cobblestones

One broke from the pack and charged out in front
It was mostly intact with its teeth ground down blunt
It snatched at our hero with fingers of steel
Wanting to make our hero its meal

With a snap and a crunch our hero's arm broke
Caught in the grips of the hungry dead folk
He felt so much pain when the zombie bit down
Perhaps he *would* die in old London town

In April Eighteen Thirty-Two
Darkness falls on me and you
Eyes that close once clearest blue
A hero dead is born anew

He heard a strong voice, gently calling his name
He tried to wake up, but no willpower came
Alone in a darkness entirely his making
He was far too exhausted to even try waking

He lay there in silence enduring the pain
Wishing that soon he could move again
Within the deep pain came a sick sort of need
A hunger for flesh and desire to feed

Then needles in skin, a hunger to slake
With his blood on the boil, he started to shake
Sweat poured from his skin and tears down his cheek
And he could not move for feeling so weak

The light burned his eyes, so he closed them tight
He only felt solace in the comfort of night
For so long he spent dreaming too long to be sure
Whether he'd died or the doc found a cure

When the pain had subsided so had the heat
And he no longer craved the taste of raw meat
His vision came back, and his strength had returned
On the monster within him the tables had turned

Soon he awoke from the nightmares and pain
Though still feeling like he'd been hit by a train
"I thought you'd been lost," said the girl with red hair
Then leaned in and kissed him leaving others to stare

"What on earth happened?" our hero exclaimed
"What made me sick and feeling so drained,"
He neglected to tell them of his hunger for meat
Instead, he picked up the cat at his feet

In April eighteen thirty-two
Our hero saved he did pull through
Not quite whole, yes this is true
It did not stop the things he'd do

A man in a coat walked up to the bed
And he handed our hero a warm piece of bread
"The answers will come so don't be afraid
Soon you will see the new hand that I made"

The man worked as well in the lab down below
They all called him turtle because he was slow
But he was quite smart and sure in his mind
And the greatest mechanic that you'd ever find

He smiled with white teeth then wandered away
Our hero had wished the turtle would stay
There were so many questions he wanted to ask
But he had gone off to complete a new task

The girl he loved stayed, and this made him smile
She was dressed in the colour of lengths of white tile
A face of sweet pink with splashings of red
That hung in loose tendrils around her sweet head

Turtle returned with a lump of cold steel
The sight of details made our poor hero reel
He looked at the place where his arm used to be
Then he closed his blue eyes so he couldn't see

He knew he'd come close to losing his life
They'd cut off his arm with a sharp butchers knife
As he looked at the thing that turtle had made
The depths of his thanks could not be conveyed

With a snap and a crunch and a very large click
He suddenly felt the arm start to tick
Like the clock and his heart, it had its own beat
And our hero felt well, and could stand on his feet

In April eighteen thirty-two
Something dark beneath the zoo
Seeps into some of the crew
And it is not a what but who

They sat at the table for dinner that night
Their cook had been clever and to their delight
A meal had been served and it was fit for kings
Or perfect for men that outrun the dead things

The only one absent which seemed out of place
The doctor decided to not show his face
They all were unnerved by the cold empty chair
Even the girl with the shiny red hair

Our hero's new claw was quite hard to use
He would've preferred that his arm he'd not lose
With a few clumsy tasks it soon moved with ease
Even while eating delicious fresh peas

Strange sounds above interrupted their meal
The return of their fears at the time was unreal
Our hero and Rob had leapt to their feet
Forsaking their meal for foes to defeat

Leaving the table and those in their chairs
Grabbing their guns, they ran for the stairs
Slowly they walked to the source of the sound
Knowing that soon there'd be horrors abound

They knew that the stairs led up to a door
No one had seen inside it before,
Now worried about what the doctor had done
They opened the door and leapt back at a run

The silence that arose from inside the room
Reminded them both of a grave to exhume
The lights on the walls were a flickering blight
Like a candle about to be snuffed in the night

In April of eighteen thirty-two
The doctor that he thought he knew
Had told him things that were untrue
About the folk who'll feast on you

From deep in the dark came a bone chilling moan
That sounded like someone in pain all alone
They stepped over the threshold and into the room
Their eyes still adjusting to the darkness and gloom

And inside there stood a few empty cages
All over the floor were books and their pages
Some of them ripped and others had burned
They all had wondered what the doctor learned

Our hero stepped forward and turned on the light
But when they could see no-one else was in sight
They then looked around for the source of the sound
And shock filled them both for what they had found

A shelf at the back that was ancient and rotting
Revealed what their friend the doctor was plotting
A map of old London had hung from the wall
Making their hiding place seem kind of small

"He was the one who started this mess!"
"He created the things, I'll make him confess,"
Rob had cried out while filling with rage
And he did not see the unemptied cage

Our hero called out; Rob spun on his feet
The thing in the cage could smell the fresh meat
It was skinny and starved, it's eyes black as pitch
And Rob swore out loud "That son of a bitch,"

"He's got one up here if it got away clean,"
And he did not dwell on what that would mean
"We've got to confront him before it gets worse
He's the one in this story that caused this foul curse."

In April eighteen thirty-two
When people put their trust in you
Lying is what's left to do
To hide from what you know is true

With one shot of his gun the creature was dead
Then leaving the room with its splatters of red
They ran down the stairs to the dining room hall
Where they found the place empty, no person at all

"They must be in bed," Rob said with despair
Our hero's scared thoughts were on the girl with red hair
"We must try to wake them, we need to get out.
Of this I am sure, there is nothing to doubt."

Our hero had hoped to call this place home
That he'd never be left on his own to roam
But the doctor did something he did not condone
And at least our brave hero was not all alone

Deep in the tunnels, to where they all sleep
The halls were now silent, not a sound, not a peep
Then one by one they woke from their dreams
To reveal the secrets of the docs evil schemes

The cook, and the turtle, the girl with red hair
Rob and our hero went back up the old stair
"The fool and a monster, the bringer of death,"
All of those names were to come in one breath

"But what to do now, we cannot just sit.
We have to get out of this horrible pit,"
Our hero looked down at the rotting undead
A new plan was forming inside of his head

"We are right to think the doctor's insane
And outside the death storm is starting to wane
But risking the monsters alone and unarmed
Is going to get one or all of us harmed."

In April eighteen thirty-two
Underneath the London Zoo
Our hero and a motley crew
Make the doctor pay his due

At first, they were worried, things started off well
They had a good plan to get out of that hell
Vengeance was second on a very short list
And theft was another important new twist

Rob and the cook got supplies they could grab
And Turtle stole things from the white tiled lab
The girl and our hero had stayed side by side
Together they searched where the doctor would hide

In passages deep, some lit by bright flame
Searching for the one they had found to blame
Soon they had come to the very last place
The door was shut tight, and it had little space

A faint ticking sound now echoed around
It seemed to come up from under the ground
They opened the door and then they both screamed
The doctor leered back, with a slack jaw he beamed

"My children, my loves, my hordes of undead,
Who eat human flesh like we eat our bread,
You're fools to believe you could ever survive,
I'm the doctor, their master, the last left alive,"

Our hero leaped forward a gun in his hand
Ready to make his very last stand,
"Yet I still breathe, blood pumps in my heart,
Our hero called out, "I'll tear you apart,"

There was a loud bang, and a very loud splat
Then came out running, the scared ginger cat
Our hero then grabbed it and looked for his foe
But the doctor was gone and where they'd not know

In April eighteen thirty-two
The dawn will bring the day anew
Just one more task to get them through
And stop the ones who'll feast on you

"Let's go," the girl said, took the cat from his arms
Then from above came the sound of alarms
As far as they could they ran through the place
Sweat from exertion all over his face

The ticking drew close and soon they'd be free
Out of the hole where the doctor would be
They saw the machine that frightened the dead
Ticking so loud and just up ahead

The turtle, the cook, and Rob were aboard
Watching so close as they ran from the horde
Our hero, and cat, the girl with red hair
Were ready and able to get out of there

The machines beating heart continued to tick
It started to move with a snap and a click
The cook he was steering, and Rob manned the gun
The girl and our hero were sure it was done

They opened the gates, heard the doctor cry out
"If you choose to escape," they all heard him shout
"The monsters will get you, at night you will see,
Your lives will be longer if you stay here with me,"

Clocks Locks Corpses!

In silence they watched as they drove through the door
The doctor could not ever settle the score
For he did not know that doors would unlock
And leave with much haste with the sound of a clock

And the corpses came out to feast on the pest
The one who'd been hurt in his very first test
On a day just like this, they finished their meal
Devoured him from his head to his heel

In May of eighteen thirty-two
Our hero found some things to do
To find more folks who made it through
And beat the ones that feast on you

This is the story but not how it ends
Our hero moved on, made many new friends
The fight was not over, and he'd never back down
There were many more monsters, in old London Town.

S. Jayne Bradley

Tad, the Vampire Slayer

More years have now passed than some care to know
It happened so fast, some wished it weren't so
The cities built tall, the sky had turned black
The world it had changed, and it couldn't turn back

Like rats in small cages, folk filled up the streets
And much bigger rats took up parliament seats
Coffers changed hands and fat cats were scratched
Their corruption and greed could not be outmatched

Soon there were plagues and illnesses spread
Half of the world's population was dead
But the buildings kept going to blot out the skies
Foundations of murder, constructed with lies

The city now lit with magenta and blue
And no one would fix what they could not undo
Slowly adapting to a world made of steel
The people began to grow and to heal

Though the sky was still dark, no stars to give light
The rumble of engines ran deep in the night
The moon now looked sick, so yellow and pale
But there was a boy who caught the wind in his sail

Clocks Locks Corpses!

In the city of codes once encrypted with blood
Encrusted with history buried deep in the mud
Those lights of magenta, of cyan, and green
Made sure that the blood on the streets had been seen

For beneath the top levels in the deep underground
Where not even worms would dare make a sound
In this city of metal, the darkness would wake
On unwary humans their thirst it will slake

And everyone knows, but nobody cares
They secretly pray for those caught unawares
For those that will wander too deep in the night
May end up alone and without any light

That is the time that afraid you should be
 There are monsters in places where people can't see
Shadows on walls and in corners of eyes
Not even the light will reveal their disguise

But one man alone with the sea in his veins
Descended the tunnels and travelled the drains
Where the light cannot reach so deep down below
He followed their tracks, and he knew where to go

While things started rough, he was quick to mature
Given a life that was hard to endure
But he was born strong and kept his head clear
Of darkness and demons, he harboured no fear

He was born in the city, not long would he dwell
To plague, death, and illness his family fell
Then off to the coast where the sea touched the sky
And the boy saw the world with an unfettered eye

A great distant uncle had taken him in
An old grizzled man with a story to spin
Beside a lagoon as the day turned to night

He taught the boy surfing, and taught him to fight

The waves were his passion and swam them he did
And soon he had grown and was no more a kid
But death came to call as it always had done
Where once he had family, the young man had none

The day had now come for he could not stay
The city was calling, and he had to obey
What his uncle had left was all that he had
Even his name, they had both chosen Tad

He packed up his things and followed the smog
The journey was long, and felt like a slog
The darkness beneath the gun metal walls
Had tugged at his dreams and he answered the calls

The place seemed familiar but not quite the same
He wasn't so sure it was right that he came
For leaving the sea to enter the gloom
Surely instead, he would find his doom

A fighter he was, and he wanted his place
No matter what monsters or ghosts he must face
There was time for reflection and changing his mind
The new world ahead, the old world behind

For the gates were now open and he would pass through
And he hoped not all tales turn out to be true
For the legends and whispers do not go untold
And he would be ready for what would unfold

He followed no path, felt wind in his hair
Whatever the road, he wouldn't despair
He knew by the sea, there were stars to alight
This thought had convinced him things would be alright

Inside the walls he had found a small place
A tiny box room with limited space
The windows were round and blocked off with bars
But it wasn't as if he could see any stars

He'd made a few friends with those who lived near
Sometimes they'd talk or crack open a beer
He told them his stories of oceans and skies
And the first and last time he'd seen the sun rise

There were deep level parties that moved with the night
They played the best music and traded in light
And Tad was distracted, and he liked it that way
They all were quite easy, and he liked to play

But he started to dream of the icy sea's touch
Of surfing and skating, he missed it so much
He'd work in the tunnels and fix up his board
It was the one thing in the world he adored

He could move like the wind on the sea and the land
If he had a board on which he could stand
And in the dark streets, and waterlogged drains
His board could roam both, the sewers, and lanes

With a new set of tools, he stepped up his game
Soon the whole world would be chanting his name
To catch on the wind, he gave it sail
For deep down below he would find a gale

Soon it was done, a machine he prepared
Whatever was broken had now been repaired
Down in the tunnels where the wind blew in hard
He took his board down to the places unbarred

It was swampy and dark with panels of switches
Contradicting the tales of lost hidden riches
A few lights that flickered was all he could find

And the roaring of winds played tricks on his mind

There were others who came to watch his first try
Joking they'd need a doctor nearby
But deep in their bones and under their skin
They were unaware of the horror within

Gathered together with the light as their shield
The strongest of tools they knew they could wield
They were all on their toes and ready to run
When Tad's first attempt was surely undone

The wind picked up speed and he opened his sail
The canvas had opened like lifting a veil
Soon he was gone so swift in the black
And the others they waited for him to come back

But the wind was too strong and carried him deep
Into the places where demons will sleep
Soon it was gone, all wind and the light
And all of his friends were far out of sight

He could not adjust to the tangible dark
Not a light in his vision not a sign or a mark
Just wide empty spaces encased in old stone
An echo of splashes and a long hollow moan

He felt for his board and crouched himself low
More horrible noises echoed up from below
A few laboured footsteps, a grinding of steel
Off of his toes he started to reel

When the sounds had still echoed and wouldn't just fade
He lifted his board, through the muck he would wade
His movement was slow and made with such care
He knew that these tunnels could lead anywhere

How far he had gone, how long would it take
These were assumptions he didn't dare make
And there in the dark, deep in that pit
The scratching and running had tested his grit

The voices grew louder, perhaps it was one
Oh what he would give for a knife or a gun
He slipped and he dragged back up the dark road
His eyes always searching for something that glowed

A sign of release escaped from his lips
When he noticed the sounds were winds and small drips
He strained with his ears and gazed in the black
Praying and hoping they wouldn't come back

He pulled on his board, and fell in the muck
And cursed the four winds, his board was now stuck
Yanking and swearing, he scraped at the wheels
Prayed to all gods, made all kinds of deals

The board wouldn't move, he'd not leave it behind
Searching for strength he doubted he'd find
But he gathered his nerves and buried his pain
He would not die here deep down in the drain

Then out of the dark came the voices once more
He dropped to his knees and kissed the damp floor
It was there in the dark to find and to feed
And Tad was in trouble, deep trouble indeed

A low horrid whisper it echoed around
A retching and gasping and gurgling sound
His hair stood on end, and held tight his breath
For the creature so near him was carrying death

The sweet sickly air on his neck had felt wet
How close it was now was making him sweat
It swirled all around him, but he could not tell

S. Jayne Bradley

What manner of creature could live in this hell

He felt the cold hand brush up his left arm
Sending out shockwaves of fear and alarm
It was not a man, nor woman, or child
Something much worse, something dark and defiled

Eternity spent waiting for its attack
While Tad stared on helplessly into the black
If he tried to run it would move for the kill
At the time it was hunting, it wanted the thrill

Circling and hungry, it cut his retreat
To it he was something quite tasty to eat
It reached out its fingers and felt for its prey
But Tad was convinced he'd not die in this way

The claws dug in deep and slashed at his skin
The sound of his whimpers called out to its kin
Just for a second, he believed he would die
And sharply and quickly with a low mewling cry

Tad struggled back but its grip was too strong
And for others to find them it wouldn't take long
The creature was writhing and twisting too quick
Coated in slime its skin was too slick

A cracked display panel threw light in the dark
And Tad for a second saw the eyes of a shark
Its jaws opened up in a snaggle toothed smile
The light was a boon, at least for a while

The panel went out and the shadows consumed
Both hunter and prey thought the other was doomed
A small voice in his thoughts had carried a fact
Of what you must do when you are attacked

Clocks Locks Corpses!

When the waters are deep, and sharks come to feed
Only one thing can help stifle their greed
Just go for the eyes his uncle would say
And then you have time to swim far away

Tad's fingers released and grabbed at its face
Ripping and tearing and scratching with grace
He felt the flesh give and sticky blood flow
Savouring savagery and taking it slow

He felt no remorse as it fell at his feet
No guilt for the wounds or his hasty retreat
The scuffle had loosed the old heavy board
He folded the sail, his wounds he ignored

From deep down below, he heard howling and screams
Not even such horrors he'd found in his dreams
For he'd looked in the eyes of the devil that day
And for murder and slaughter there'd be hell to pay

Woozy and weary he re-joined the city
But now he looked on with a strong sense of pity
The people wore masks, they'd not see, or hear
It was an illusion, and they lived in fear

The tunnels had ended in an old subway train
He limped and he struggled, enduring the pain
The scars would be great, a battle was won
But this terrible war had only begun

He knew where they lived and the way that they fed
He'd soon find the ways to make them all dead
Help wasn't needed if he timed it all right
He promised himself there'd be bloodshed that night

He fled the dark subway with skateboard in tow
More scrapings and howling had come from below
He'd gone way off course the distance was far

If it had been much further, he'd have needed a car

Over some boxes and an old broken gate
As if catching a train for which he was late
He lifted his board and dragged it behind
And decided it had been quite poorly designed

The sounds from below had suddenly stopped
Alone in the dark the wind also dropped
Out of the drain and out of the damp
He limped onto the street and under a lamp

It should have been quiet at this time of night
But the city it breathed, and it heaved a false light
The chase it was over and new wounds would heal
New ways of living and thoughts to congeal

He remembered the thing in the dark and the deep
The memory meant he could not fall asleep
For he saw them again each time his eyes closed
And what kind of world would he see when he dozed

The sky thundered and rolled in blackening coils
Covered in smoke and reeking of oils
It was no surprise that evil would thrive
In a place where the humans were barely alive

He took a deep breath to slow down his heart
But the smell and the taste it tore him apart
And as the fog cleared from the edge of his vision
About this old city he made a decision

Magenta and cyan were bright in his eyes
Second only to oceans that meet with the skies
The city itself was a beacon of change
But now an ideal too far out of range

Perhaps being close to winding up dead
Makes life more worthy of living instead
He shivered a little as a bus rumbled by
Some girls wandered passed and gave him the eye

Some things were memories and others were new
The steel and the stone, magenta and blue
It was darkness and light, and down in the drain
This muck and the black was the Vampires domain

A hand grabbed his arm and gave him a shock
He almost spun round and gave them a knock
It was one of his friends who was there for his ride
To find him she promised they really had tried

They knew of the danger, but the risk was too high
For Tad's reckless act, not one soul should die
He felt some remorse for the dangerous run
And the things that he saw were not worth the fun

His friend took the board and helped him back home
The streets at that time were a danger to roam
He patched up his wounds and washed off the mud
Washed off the dust the slime and the blood

There were no broken bones but his clothes were all torn
In places not ripped the fabrics were worn
He stared at his face reflected in steel
A lesson was learned to spite his ordeal

He lay on his bed, but the drain called his name
Creatures of memory from, darkness they came
In a moment of weakness, he gave himself flack
So this time he would be prepared for the black

In silence he worked on fixing his board
All contact with friends, his screens were ignored
He did not explain of what had occurred

To hide what he'd seen was simply preferred

He stocked up on things that burn and explode
And downed a cold beer, just one for the road
To just disappear, in the pipes he would go
No-one was aware of his hunt for this foe

There was something else that he understood
His board unrepaired was simply no good
He polished it up and fixed up the sail
With an added harpoon he just couldn't fail

The next step was blindness, he needed to see
For night vision goggles he paid a small fee
He added some rope and also a knife
It was a small thing between death and his life

A fresh lick of paint and old fabrics dyed
Knowing like them he'd be able to hide
And when it was done, he started to smile
He was decked out for speed, for danger, and style

Deep in the night he locked up his room
And slipping on out all alone in the gloom
The city was teaming with man and machine
And he moved through the streets so swift and unseen

He travelled back down to the old subway car
From his apartment it wasn't that far
He set up his things by the way he had come
Hiding behind an old oil drum

The wind was not moving, and neither was he
With night vision on he waited to see
He was sure they'd come out in a moment or two
A blood bath of vampires would surely ensue

For that's what was hiding deep under the ground
Feeding on blood, not making a sound
He had heard the rumours and thought they were lies
So, seeing them there had been a surprise

Now he was waiting for them to find him
That thought made his chances indeed very slim
There'd be a fair few of the creatures he sought
But he'd remain strong so he could say that he fought

As he counted down seconds they came into sight
Dark hair and eyes and skin of off white
There were six of them there and all very thin
Each of them wore a pointed tooth grin

The first two were women fine boned and fair
Each of them had long, shiny black hair
Subtle, demure with a fine set of hips
But fangs pointed over their pretty red lips

To him they were deadly but beauties no less
How old or how young he never could guess
Their movements were fluid and so full of grace
In a city like this they were not out of place

But their eyes had no mirth they were soulless and cold
No clue to what devil their souls had been sold
When scrutinized close their ill look was known
The clothes just hung off them, they were all skin and bone

Tad had to turn and look at the others
They were all alike and possibly brothers
Seemingly thin like the women appeared
Strikingly handsome but something felt weird

Alien, human and something between
Decidedly loathsome, so foul and unclean
Immaculate clothing, without any stains

Strange and unnerving for things from the drains

What soul had been lost while treading off route
For the sake of their style of a fashionable suit
Their buttons were shining, a glimmer of brass
Clearly these things were once upper class

It seemed a real shame, to destroy such good taste
To ruin good suits was a terrible waste
But the deed must be done, and blood must be shed
The monsters and demons they have to be dead

It was then that he saw one was heavily scarred
Clearly the one with which Tad had once sparred
Its flesh hadn't healed, its eye sockets black
But being unsighted did not hold it back

But pity was lost in an unending hate
Tad knew he must strike before it was too late
So, he braced himself down and let his rage fly
Today was a good day, a great day to die

The harpoon went first, straight into the chest
Of one of the men who was wearing a vest
He fell to his knees and turned into ash
The others then screeched but were gone in a flash

For a moment a silence surrounded his frame
A small sense of triumph it suddenly came
One was now dead with five more to go
And if there were more, he sure didn't know

He gathered his things and followed their trail
Riding the board with the wind in his sail
 One disappeared around a sharp bend
He had to be quick or in the landscape she'd blend

The scrape of his wheels were lost in the sound
Of the trains and the buses so far above ground
He saw her pass by through a gap in the wall
Then it was as if she'd not been there at all

For a second he thought he was playing their game
And running him ragged was a part of their aim
They probably knew he was there all along
His once cunning plan turned out to be wrong

With his laser gun loaded and ready to fire
He found himself lagging and starting to tire
But he pushed himself on and continued the chase
And when he would find them he'd aim for the face

It was then that he saw her on a maintenance stair
Moaning and weeping and pulling her hair
She looked up at Tad with such horror and hate
And if she'd been human was up for debate

He felt some remorse as he lifted his gun
But she bared her fangs, and the fight had begun
A flash of blue light rushed into her eyes
She thrashed and she spat and let out shrill cries

Blackish grey blood had dripped down her cheeks,
Her slow painful death would haunt him for weeks
One final shot, direct to her chest
She crumbled to ash, and he went for the rest

Four more to go, their locations unknown
Many places to hide in steel and in stone
A lifetime of searching, he'd not find all six
This wasn't a problem just one day could fix

Turning around to make his way back
But another was staring at him from the black
A foul twisted scowl that could curdle fresh milk

Forgetting the fact he was dressed in fine silk

Between them there was a palpable tension
And all of time seemed to be in suspension
He fired his gun and missed every shot
In a flash it was there, and then it was not

Firing blindly, turning round and around
The crashing of trash made a hell of a sound
Its cold sneering face peering left and then right
And then in a flash it had vanished from sight

Tad was left standing, a chill on his skin
He waited in vain for the assault to begin
For the night was not over and deep underground
In the tunnels and drains they'd be found

Under his breath he cursed and he swore
He doubted that he could withstand anymore
The risk was too high, the danger too real
It was his own doom that he would soon seal

In a flash it was there, its mouth open wide
Its teeth they were gleaming, and it showed them with pride
Tad fired his gun with a mind to cause harm
The shot it struck bone in the monster's right arm

Spurts of black blood sprayed out from the hole
It screamed and it cried, the wound took its toll
Assuring himself that the beast would be slain
Tad fired his gun but missed once again

It made a shrill laugh, a dead hollow shriek
Declaring that Tad was useless and weak
That his life would soon end in the most painful way
And he would regret all his actions this day

But Tad had ignored the vampire's lies
He could see right through the fear in its eyes
The creature recoiled, the action it shows
The weaker it is the louder it crows

It leaped from his perch with his arms duly raised
Its form and its speed could only be praised
For seconds uncounted Tad was frozen in place
This moment of weakness he'd love to efface

A voice from his past he heard in his head
Diverting the fear with what it had said
When out on the waves and wind had been strong
And he had been out for ever so long

Arms both were shaking, and too tired to row
And so far from shore the tide wasn't low
His uncle explained and warned him each day
That surfing alone was just not the way

Danger and death could arrive any time
To act without thought was almost a crime
But if you were stuck, too tired and frail
To lift up your spirits, rely on your sail

In a flash Tad had swung his board to his aid
Transforming its sail into a sharp blade
Too late to evade, Tad's movements were true
The sail then impaled it, running right through

In triumph Tad cried as the vampire fell
And sent it back into its own pit in hell
The sail was now broken but he didn't care
Another dark creature was ash in the air

Just three more to go, he was halfway complete
And soon everyone would be safe on the street
No more murders, or blood, or fear of the night

S. Jayne Bradley

The war was half over, and the outlook was bright

Tad now believed that he would win this game
And all of the world would soon know his name
As he stood there with pride at his feet was his kill
A blood curdling scream was heard deeper still

He knew that sound well so off he did skate
With a bloodsucking ghoul he had a hot date
The wind in his hair on uneven ground
To the aid of the screamer at great speed was bound

The lights of magenta, of cyan and green
A panel display had lit up the scene
As he rounded a bend the danger he viewed
A woman in pink was being subdued

From far up above she'd clearly been taken
Tad met her wide eyes, she'd not be forsaken
In his search it had time to steal from above
And he'd take her place if push came to shove

He had to act fast before it could feed
And towards them he rode and gathered his speed
In his one hand a gun, the other a knife
He'd rescue the girl at the risk of his life

The city light glowed in magenta and blue
And what had been done they could not undo
The darkness prevailed and every new turn
The war had been lost and no-one would learn

It was a bad dream of which no-one would wake
Filled with these demons in a hellish outbreak
Perpetual night except by the sea
Where the filth had not spread like a rot in a tree

But Tad had soon learned that nothing stays clean
No part of the world could stay so pristine
Unless things were done to cancel the spread
His home and his ocean would soon wind-up dead

And it's asked quite a lot what one man can do
To stop the disease from breaking on through
The truth of the monsters that feed in the dark
Would cause the explosion by lighting the spark

All this he thought as he rode to her aid
It's in moments like these where horrors are made
No thoughts of himself as he cried out for war
Ready for the death, the blood, and the gore

Onto its back he leaped from his board
For a moment or two like an eagle he soared
The knife in his hand he jabbed in its side
He clung to its neck like an old bronco ride

Stabbing again as it sprayed out black blood
They both toppled over and into the mud
Tad saw the lights that had reeled overhead
The skin of his foes he had started to shred

His knife then struck home, its ribs made a crack
The creature cried out as its body went slack
The woman looked on in shock and surprise
She did not believe what she saw with her eyes

She bent down to help Tad onto his feet
He stood up and smiled, she was as white as a sheet
She thanked him profusely for saving her neck
And offered rewards by writing a cheque

He declined the kind offer and she asked for his name
He shook his head as he didn't want fame
For his duty required him not to be known

Or into the vampires grasp he'd be thrown

Tad then skated off after helping her home
For there was still danger in this city of chrome
By the time she had gone it was too late for more
He doubted they were within reach anymore

Exhaustion and fear were claiming his brain
Though his thoughts were now on the two that remain
He knew he would find them it had to be done
And riding the sewers he'd admit, it was fun

He wound his way through the city, the maze
Tired and aching, his mind in a daze
Though dark was the sky it was closer to dawn
Despite all his protests he started to yawn

Glad he was safe for the light that was growing
Some strength he found in the mere fact of knowing
Four were now dead, but soon there'd be more
Sooner or later they'd be at his door

With weapons a plenty so close by his side
With many more hunters there'd be nowhere to hide
A purging of darkness and light would return
But in this beginning there was no concern

For now it was bed and then maybe he'd eat
And still feeling bad for the task incomplete
But night would return, and they would give chase
And that didn't mean he'd be leaving this place

For the dead at his hand had faded to dust
The blood hungry fiends filled him with disgust
But there would be more for him to destroy
And he knew that each kill he would always enjoy

Clocks Locks Corpses!

He entered his building and felt some relief
But this moment of peace for him would be brief
He remembered when leaving he'd locked the front door
This turn of events was no game anymore

He withdrew his gun and paused for a breath
Best he relax before facing his death
And as he was sure that it knew he was there
If he didn't slow down, he knew how he'd fare

Touching the steel of the door in his way
Keeping his fear of the monster at bay
Over the threshold and into the room
The battle for now Tad would have to resume

A whisper of memory once lost to his past
Returned to his conscious thinking at last
A dear uncle's voice as clear as the day
Forestalling the moment and causing delay

In moments of strength when triumph is had
It is at that time that things can go bad
Be humble and brave and watch what you do
Just one small mistake and all plans can fall through

The door closed behind he was ready to fight
As if things were normal he turned on the light
He took a few steps, saw the creature was there,
Its back to the door in the only arm chair

Tad did not speak; no words had been needed
His uncle's old warning he'd certainly heeded
It sat there in wait for first moves to be made
But Tad wasn't worried, he wasn't afraid

The chair turned around and with a sick smile
That was not at all happy and somewhat hostile
But it wasn't the thing that caused him surprise

It was the first vampire, Tad had taken his eyes

On closer inspection, it had not healed well
How much damage he'd done, now Tad he could tell
For both eyes were gone, just scars now remained
The veins on its neck were bulging and strained

It breathed in so deep through its mouth and its nose
And then from the chair the vampire rose
Still in its suit and hair had been styled
It clicked its long fingers and no longer smiled

Tad lifted his gun and slowly he aimed
To miss at this range would make him ashamed
Everything slowed, in a flash the gun fired
But what he had hoped was not what transpired

The vampire had strength, more strength than its friends
On how he would fight, his life now depends
In a flash it had moved right out of the way
Letting the blast from his gun go astray

It laughed at the fumble, a black hollow sound
In a single swift move it pushed Tad to the ground
It reached with a hand and grasped at his throat
And with a free hand, Tad grabbed at its coat

He felt its hot breath on his neck and his face
Tad knew that he had to break this embrace
He kicked and he thrashed, and he tried to flail
But the wind had completely gone out of his sail

Darkness had crept to the edges of sight
Magenta and blue now held back the night
The vampire's breath had burned like hot coal
It wanted his blood, and it wanted his soul

No more would he hunt or ride with the wind
The monster would bite as he lay there pinned
For him to give up was so easy to do
The lights were so soothing, magenta, and blue

The cool ocean waves, they crashed in his ears
He saw the blue skies for the first time in years
His uncle's voice called him faint but so strong
He'd see him again, it wouldn't be long

But in his mind's eye there was a red glow
Deep in a place that he did not know
His fingers held fast to what he'd remember
He felt his hope grow like a hot fiery ember

It swam into view, and he understood
Meeting death here would not do any good
He reached for his gun and felt the cold steel
Hoping he would not end up as a meal

It was him and the vampire and a gun in between
The trigger he pulled in flash of blue green
Howling in pain, it rolled on the floor
Clutching its guts, it made for the door

Onto his feet he leapt with great speed
He gathered his strength for his hour of need
Three times he fired to take down his foe
It would never go back to sewers below

As it then turned it whispered his name
Then a pile of dust the creature became
Taken aback, Tad reversed a few feet
Despite this blind vampire's crushing defeat

It knew of his name which meant others did
He wouldn't be safe, and not if he hid
Others would come, of that he was sure

A new fact of life he had to endure

The pile of dust on the carpet it stained
The vampires, attack had left him so drained
He counted one more that had slipped his wrath
But this was a case of more than just math

If one was still free, there would be lots more
Would probably come right to his front door
The danger was greater, but he didn't mind
It just made it easier to leave things behind

He knew he must go, but not to the sea
The city was where he needed to be
He gathered his board and a few other things
This surfer and skater was about to grow wings

Life in the city would always be hard
In all these new places, he'd be on his guard
Sadly, his friends he must leave behind
To drag them along, it would be unkind

Part of him wished to wait out his days
Living in style in a bright ocean haze
But he knew it unwise, there was work to be done
He wanted the dark, but he needed the sun

A turn in his life, he did not expect
He took a few seconds to think and reflect
For the road he would take would suit him just fine
Magenta and blue, in his life they would shine

But deep in the pipes their numbers would grow
In a city of darkness where the wind would still blow
In silence he'd move from section to section
Purging this place of the demon infection

The black blood will flow with ash in the breeze
He'll slaughter them all and do it with ease
No vampiric soul could ever survive
At least they'll not live while he is alive

He closed the front door with one look inside
To take his old life and cast it aside
He'll fix up his board and take to the road
Without a complaint he'll carry the load

The world was now changing, and light would soon show
And everything else would go with the flow
Not a usual man or a regular player
He was now Tad, the Vampire Slayer.

Rock'n'Roll Cyborg

Chapter 1

A great beating heart
The size of a clock
Moulded with steel
And sealed with a lock

Silver and chrome
Gold, copper, and brass
Creating from sand
Eyes of stained glass

The smith had worked hard
To build and to learn
A fiery furnace
With hot coal to burn

And ever it seemed
He'd be in his store
Selling off toys
And building some more

But there was one thing
He loved over all
His son, a tall man,
Was not man at all

But still incomplete
So much he must make
For the heart to beat
Blink brown eyes awake

A delicate thing
He kept locked away
Others would want him
And would find a way

He'll be a Rock'n'Roll Cyborg
He'll learn how to ride
He's a metal made android
With a soft hidden side

Chapter 2

The maker was old
Beyond Middle Age
Had worked his whole life
For minimum wage

But he knew his stuff
And he knew he was smart

He brought a new meaning
To the metal work art

Stains on his clothes
Grease on his cheeks
Into his workshop
He'd vanish for weeks

An idea had come
When his child had died
An event that had cost
His love and his pride

He'd make a new man
Out of iron and steel
He'd teach it to think
And teach it to feel

He'd gotten so far
It was almost complete
It could blink its own eyes
And walk on its feet

It still could not speak
And words would come slow
And there were some things
It just didn't know

He'll be a rock n roll cyborg
Who will learn and grow
He's a metal made android
But he's still very slow

Chapter 3

The workshop had tools
Of so many sorts
Some made of metal
And others of quartz

They were finely polished
And gleamed in the light
The maker was prepping
To work through the night

The clinking of hammers
Could be heard all around
As the maker had worked
To this task he was bound

The lights shone so bright
Upon the large bench
The maker leaned over
And clutched at his wrench

On the table he laid
The cyborg of steel
His body stayed still
Its form was ideal

Smooth skin of silver
In bright light it shines
Showing the details
Of the makers designs

But there was no life
In those agate brown eyes
The maker had asked
For him not to rise

He'll be a Rock'n'Roll Cyborg
Who will know how to dance
He'll be a metal made android
If he's given the chance

Chapter 4

The lights flickered off
He knew who had come
The lights on the cyborg
Had made him feel numb

He turned on his torch
And continued to build
Taking the risk
That he might be killed

Footsteps on ceilings
Crunching on floors
Soon they'd come in
By breaking the doors

But still he kept working
His will surpassed need
He knew that their mercy
Would not surpass greed

The maker heard creaking
As they hurried in
A secret door opened
The cyborg within

And on the workbench
He had hit his head

The popping of guns
The maker was dead

All was now dark
As they took his stuff
They'd not take the cyborg
But they'd take enough

He's a Rock'n'Roll Cyborg
Who will wake up soon
He's a metal made android
Waking up with the moon

Chapter 5

He remembered the dark
And the quiet and cold
He remembered the maker
And a glitter of gold

There was a soft tick
He knew was his heart
And it had been there
From right at the start

As time pushed on past
He started to think
He started to move
And started to blink

The secret door opened
He stepped slowly out
He'd call for his maker
But he could not shout

Clocks Locks Corpses!

The images played
Behind his brown eyes
He tried to make sense
Of the who's and the why's

A stain on the floor
A deep vibrant red
The cyborg then saw
That his maker was dead

Then without thought
He knew what to do
He pulled on some clothes
And checked out the view

He's a Rock'n'Roll Cyborg
With his own kind of style
He's a metal made android
And he's here for a while

Chapter 6

Alone in the house
And lots to explore
He left the workshop
To get a grand tour

Something was stuck
Emotions came slow
But where he would go
He did seem to know

To the shed he was drawn
Like a moth to a flame
He felt a connection

Machines were the same

The shed soon opened
It was dark inside
He reached for the switch
The light now his guide

That's when the light
All yellow and green
Revealed the best thing
That he'd ever seen

It glowed and it gleamed
And longed for his touch
He reached out a hand
And fingered the clutch

He admired the wheels
The tyres he stroked
Oh, the grand feelings
The cycle invoked

He's a rock'n'roll Cyborg
Who knows what he'll like
He's a metal made android
With a motorbike

Chapter 7

A rumble of engines
Smoke from behind
This rock'n'roll cyborg
Has now been defined

Its make fits him well

It's just the right size
Such a beautiful thing
For his agate brown eyes

The night was still young
He was newly born
In a jacket and jeans
So artfully torn

Rebel on highways
Android on roads
Kicking some ass
In binary codes

He won't feel the wind
The cold he'll not know
But he knows how to ride
And he does, like a pro

The streets were empty
And free of all cars
For the first time ever
He could see the stars

The bike feels connected
Like it's now part of him
A duplicate soul
A heart and a limb

He is a Rock'n'Roll Cyborg
So sure where he'd go
He is a metal made android
And he'll not get there slow

Chapter 8

Rides like the lightning
Through the dark city
Looking at lights
For they were so pretty

Red and Blue flashes
Had followed him around
Long and low the song
Unfamiliar sound

The lights glowing bright
Trying to get near
Pulling out in front
Causes him to veer

He just kept on riding
Picking up his speed
The motorbike was fast
He was in the lead

They were just some lights
That just wanted to play
He had no time for games
He did not want to stay

He liked all the colours
On his skin they shined
Distracted by the flashing
For a moment he was blind

The bike got in a skid
He lost all control
With a crunch and smash
Wrapped around a pole

He is a rock'n'roll Cyborg
Who knew how to fall
He is a metal made android
Who's not hurt at all

Chapter 9

A furnace of flame
He was caught in fire
This situation
Became very dire

But soon he emerged
Climbed from the wreck
The policemen just stared
One scratching his neck

He picked up his bike
Ignoring the heat
And all of the cops
Were white as a sheet

They looked on in awe
Not believing their eyes
They saw he was steel
It was a surprise

The cyborg climbed on
And though it was scratched
He revved up the engine
The cops were outmatched

The cyborg then fixed
A very large dent

Twisted the wheels
Where they had been bent

It was slightly better
And he knew it would go
But he had not thought
Cops would be in tow

He's a Rock 'n' Roll Cyborg
With a cast iron jaw
He's a metal made android
In a fix with the law

Chapter 10

They were all shouting loudly
He didn't know why
There were like ten cops
And three passers by

The fear rose within them
His skin glowed with fire
He never felt heat
Or sensed the town's ire

He could hear them all shout
And their horns were tooting
He started to move
And they started shooting

The bullets bounced off
And fell to the ground
There were dents in his skin
And a loud pinging sound

The heat and the feel
He didn't much like
He decided to leave
So, he revved up the bike

The engine it roared
It kicked into gear
He left them in dust
He got himself clear

The bike sped away
The cops would give chase
They started thinking
It was more of a race

He's a Rock 'n' Roll Cyborg
With the cops in a run
He's a metal made android
And he's having such fun

Chapter 11

Through back roads and
streets
Through alleys and lanes
Then passing under
Overpasses for trains

Through traffic and lots
Without slowing down
In a flash he had seen
The whole of the town

The cops shot their guns
As they tried to get near

But the cyborg ignored them
Kicked into high gear

There was nowhere to run
And nowhere to hide
It was also much harder
To stay on his ride

He avoided blockades
Pedestrians too
And now he was lost
Unsure what to do

There were dents in his bike
Where bullets had struck
Now he thought sadly
He was out of luck

He would now escape
The distance would grow
If they could keep up
He had no way to know

He's a Rock 'N' Roll Cyborg
And he is faster than light
He's a metal made Android
Who will race through the
night

Chapter 12

Soon there were no lights
No sirens or shots
Silence descended
On these parking lots

His engine had stalled
His gas was now low
If he was to make it
He'd have to go slow

The sky was so dark
And lit up with stars
He listened for sirens
And the rumble of cars

But late in the night
All humans asleep
The cyborg he waited
As he sat in a heap

His mind was now working
On things he had seen
The things he had done
And all lights were green

Vaguely he heard them
So distant a sound
Sure they were hunting
But he'd not be found

He was too far away
And so he remained
And sat all alone
His energy drained

He is a Rock 'n' Roll Cyborg
Alone in the dark
He is a metal made Android
Where others will park

Chapter 13

Nine in the morning
When he opened his store
A shock of a lifetime
Was at his front door

Just a mechanic
Who works nine to five
Had never seen metal
That could be alive

Mechanic by trade
Wires on his brains
A lifetime of wrenches
And oil in his veins

Though he was young
He sure knew his trade
Took pride in his work
And all he had made

The cyborg just sat there
In a heap by the door
The cyborg and cycle
Weren't alone anymore

For a moment he thought
He was still in his bed
That this was a dream
Formed inside his head

But it shone in the light
It appeared to be real

A new motorbike
And the man made of steel

He saw a Rock 'n' Roll Cyborg
Who had learned how to ride
He saw a metal made Android
And he brought him inside

Chapter 14

The bike needed work
But not very much
He couldn't just look
He wanted to touch

The man didn't move
So he left it alone
And if it would wake
It'd wake on its own

To fix up the bike
Would be his first task
He wasn't a thief
Though he didn't ask

He buffed out the scratches
Gave the engine a tune
And then he was done
By mid afternoon

The paint was retouched
And then left to dry
And when it was done
He let out a sigh

He turned to the Cyborg
So much to be done
The dents he was sure
Were dents from a gun

He examined details
It couldn't be fake
And then in a flash
The man was awake

He was a Rock 'n' Roll Cyborg
With agate brown eyes
Woke a metal made android
And got it to rise

Chapter 15

He reached out to touch
So alive and so cold
He'd never believed it
If he had been told

Light bounced off the steel
On his chest and face
And he could now see
Its beauty and grace

A panel then opened
A screen in its chest
On display could be seen
An old family crest

A recording then played
For man and machine
His makers last hours
By both could be seen

He told them a story
Of how he was made
A promise of payment
That had never been paid

They wanted the plans
And they had the power
So they took it all
In his very last hour

They got what they wanted
And carried no debt
With the maker now dead
Their future was set

Plans for a Rock 'n' Roll
Cyborg
Were stolen that day
And a metal made android
would make those men pay

Chapter 16

Because he was hidden
He had not been found
For when they had come
He'd not been around

The maker was killed
And he knew what to do

He did not know fear
But hatred he knew

Revenge would be his
And stop what they planned
The mechanic was ready
To lend him a hand

So he would be mended
And sent on his way
The thieves and a killer
They now had to pay

The scratches now buffed
And panels all clean
After hours of work
Its skin had a sheen

No scorch marks or dents
Were left on his skin
The mechanic was pleased
So he started to grin

His closet was raided
For clothes that would suit
A fine leather jacket
And a guitar to boot

He was a Rock 'n' Roll Cyborg
With death on his mind
He was a metal made android
The villains he'd find

Chapter 17

And then on the news
He saw his own face
In the centre of town
In a long police chase

The mechanic then stared
And gave him a name
For a chase he'd escaped
And earned him his fame

They started their search
To hunt down their foe
For a crime was committed
By who they don't know

Time they had plenty
For help they would need
They must find the man
Who had done the deed

The mechanic had friends
A crew you could say
And each had their strengths
In their own special way

Some had been Bikers
Some rode on still
Others mechanics
Had steel for their skill

And so they had joined
For a murderer hunt
Out on their bikes
With a Cyborg out front

He was a Rock 'n' Roll Cyborg
With an army in tow
He was a metal made android
Who will hunt down his foe

Chapter 18

More facts had been found
At his maker's work shop
With a long list of names
That led right to the top

The mechanic was shocked
By what they had found
For a very long time
He had not made a sound

Then off on their hunt
They soon had returned
Knowing these monsters
Would have to be burned

On bright shining bikes
In the hot summer sun
They arrive at town hall
With a job to be done

The sky was so blue
Reflected in steel
And he glittered so bright
That he didn't seem real

A day of bad omens
Of battles unfought
The danger was growing
But wasn't for naught

Each had their weapon
And each knew their role
The murderer's payment
The ultimate goal

He was a Rock 'n' Roll Cyborg
With a hard road ahead
He was metal made Cyborg
To the future he sped

Chapter 19

The town hall was huge
And they parked at the front
This was the ending
To the murderer hunt

Vengeance was coming
The debt to be paid
For the life of a man
That had been betrayed

They called out their foe
Each name had been given
Until out of the doors
New androids were driven

A new kind of army
Had been made of chrome
From the maker's own plans

They took from his home

They hummed and they
rumbled
Like a large swarm of bees
Spewing black smoke
Into the cool breeze

They did not look human
Had guns on each side
The bikers hung back
They'd nowhere to hide

Wall to wall monsters
Of flame and of steel
And much braver men
Would turn on their heel

He is a Rock 'n' Roll Android
Who knows of the plan
He is a metal made android
Who'll do what he can

Chapter 20

Their numbers were huge
Steel boots shook the ground
A roar and a rumble
There was danger around

Guns were then fired
And things set alight
Bikers with helmets
Had pitched for a fight

With crowbars they swung
And bats they made strikes
The air filled with smoke
And the sound of their bikes

But there were so many
Against them a wall
And it took so much
To get one to fall

There was blood and oil
And fires would catch
The bikers they knew
They had met their match

The time had now come
For a quick retreat
But this was no loss
It was no defeat

For the Cyborg was ready
As a new message played
They stared at his chest
Saw what was displayed

He is a Rock 'n' Roll Cyborg
Who played his first bar
He is a metal made Android
Who pulled out his guitar

Chapter 21

In numbers bright green
In a countdown from ten
It would not take much

For what happened then

The bikers had fled
At a distance they saw
His guitar was singing
They all watched in awe

The countdown went on
In an eight counts of four
And within that town hall
Not a soul anymore

It had all exploded
Destroyed those who stayed
And falling to dust
His part was now played

The danger abated
The tables had turned
And in smoke and fire
The bikers returned

The flames burning bright
The sky had turned grey
The bikers would mourn
Their friend's deaths that day

Schematics now lost
No more would be made
For all human life
He had made a trade

He was a Rock 'n' Roll Cyborg
Who knew of his place
He was a metal made android
Who saved the human race

Chapter 22

No-one could get closer
Until the smoke cleared
They saw all his parts
And was just as they feared

Piles of scrap metal
Lay strewn all around
And their cyborg friend
A burned metal mound

His body in pieces
He was melted and burned
And which part was what
Could not been discerned

The others were broken
Destroyed in the blow
They'd been built so fast
And how they'd not know

With great bags in hand
They gathered the bits
And scanning each piece
To see how it fits

Focused on the task
They had to beat the cops
Taking what was left

To their auto shops

The mechanic was sad
He'd lost this fine art
Never had there been
machines
That had souls as a part

He was a Rock 'n' Roll Cyborg
Who saved the human race
He was a metal made android
Whose given name was Chase

Chapter 23

The store had closed early
Repairs must be made
The damage extensive
And he did not want aid

Meticulous working
Many pieces replaced
The work was not easy
No plans had been traced

This always was a challenge
A long road with twists
There were many problems
Some were solved with fists

Chase the Cyborg was broken
He had to be fixed
The mechanic would try
And results would be mixed

S. Jayne Bradley

He was unafraid,
This master of steel
He promised the cyborg
That he'd be made real

Schematics in dreams
Metal on the brains
Working day and night
He earned all his stains

He knew how to fix him
He had all the tools
To give up was easy
For losers and for fools

He was a Rock 'n' Roll Cyborg
Whose circuits were fried
He is a metal made android
Whose eyes opened wide

Secret Stills

There is a shelf, in one small store
It's been there since the great world war
Unless you know where you must look
You'll never see what's in that nook,

The shop is in a tiny town
Where dirt is grey, the grass is brown
City roads don't reach its edge
Between these worlds there is a wedge

The ancient hills they pierce the sky,
Unless they're cut, the trees don't die
Sunsets shine with golds and green
The moon is bright, and stars are seen

But shifting shadows skulk and lurk
And tromping boots behove the work
In places where the sun won't go
Where myths are born and fireflies glow

The morning comes and with it dread
Without a warning being said
An engine sound once distant near
And it's the harbinger of fear

He came from steel and concrete places

S. Jayne Bradley

From cities with so many faces
He would come here, uphold the laws
With silver tongue and snapping jaws

His car was new and shone so bright
It filled the residents with fright
And with such care his engine ceased
The locals knew this kind of beast

His suit was grey just like his eyes
The badge that's waved is no surprise
The general store had opened wide
This DA would not be denied

He had his names and orders true
And it was clear what he would do
The rumours of the secret stills
Had brought this man toward the hills

An old man nears with pipe in hand
With one cocked hip he takes a stand
"Y'all not welcome here that's sure
You bring a stink worse than manure."

The DA smiled and lit a smoke
The man backed down no words were spoke
Shark like eyes had pushed him back
This city boy would soon attack

The store doors creaked as he stepped in
With icy eyes and hungry grin,
He scanned the shelves for things to catch
A plan had grown, about to hatch

Clocks Locks Corpses!

The owner stood with hands on hips
Her teeth were clenched behind chapped lips
"I hope you're here to order stuff,"
Her tone was clipped, her voice was rough

He had seen what he desired,
And watched her as her brow perspired
His hand reached out, so pale and prim
His jaw was set, his face was grim

"Tell me ma'am what's in the jar,
And lying will not get you far,"
The woman frowned and dropped her gaze
Presumption he would have to praise

When moon is blue, and stars are bright
The moonshine flows throughout the night
The clouds do clear, and trees will bow
The question's never where but how

He sniffed the jar and knew it well
He knew what she'd been trying to sell
Her face was grey, and jaw was slack
He raised his hand and gave a smack

She sang of hills and mountain trails
Of secrets deep in glades and vales
A mark she bore for secrets told
She'd wear it 'til she would grow old

With rumpled suit and knuckles cut
Behind him had he heard doors shut
He left the town with truth in hand
He'd grab his troops and scour the land

S. Jayne Bradley

Three days passed and he came back
Three more troopers to help him track
The shop was closed all stock was lost
He knew it had been at her cost

The car doors slammed, and guns were loaded
The DA hoped they'd not be goaded
They felt the eyes of those unseen
And he was glad to keep things clean

They found the trail into the hills
Their hunt began for secret stills
A marker sat upon a post
A horse head skull white like a ghost

It stared at them with empty eyes
As if to judge them for their lies
So on they went with bones now ice
And hoped that courage would suffice

As they marched through bush and tree
No human print could their eyes see
As if each man had rode a horse
But that was just so mad of course

But on they trekked on smallest trail
And hunted, but to no avail
Their quarry seemed just out of sight
And soon they'd be alone at night

Sometime when the moon would rise
And light would soon face its demise
The troopers watched the stars alight
So would they flee, or would they fight?

Clocks Locks Corpses!

And then the horses' hooves they heard
The troopers never said a word
As horses came, with barrels full
And strange enough no carts to pull

The DA stared with mouth hung wide
His troopers had then fled his side
As horse and rider moved as one
He straightened up and raised his gun

No shot rang out, no fleeing birds
His soul cried out, "They move in herds"
They stared at him with jewel bright eyes
The horses' prints were no disguise

Stood eighteen hands from tip to tail
The DA'd not get them to jail
They raised their spear then knocked him down
He doubted he'd get back to town

He thought he could just cease their still
But now he seemed to lack the will
Their eyes and blades had glinted bright
He wasn't going home that night

Tall and proud these creatures moved
Despite the fact they were all hooved
One watched the DA get too near
Its eyes were wide, its face was clear

It tried to show they'd do no harm
The DA stood and grabbed its arm
Its anger rose, and eyes turned black
The DA gasped and stumbled back

S. Jayne Bradley

The Centaurs marched between the trees
Left him alone to cough and wheeze
No other cop had seen their eyes
Or what secret in the mountain lies

Off to town when morning came
And every soul had learned his name
Suit once grey and hair so slick
Was caked with mud and grass so thick

He looked deranged, his eyes were wild
He spoke and acted like a child
When the tale he told was spun
It proved that his career was done

No one believed the things he'd seen
He'd leave the hills and trees of green
And home he went, to then forget
What he saw and who he met

The moonshine flowed from secret stills
From glades and vales within the hills
From water pure and grains of course
Made by neither man nor horse

The Union Man

A man of sixty, ashen face
He struggles to keep up the pace
Hands are cracked with age and pain
He fumbles with his knife again

The whistle blows, Bill takes a breath
Staving off the hand of death
Eight more hours, six complete
But he has not yet felt defeat.

The bossman stalks along the line
Counting steer and counting swine
Wearing boots, the workers tanned
And on their backs with boots he'll stand

His tongue is sharp, Bill's skin is thick
He knows that he can take a lick
No iron fist will break his spine
He'll keep his place upon the line

The Boss, they knew he was not right
But in Bill's head, they could not fight,
All workers thought their worth was low
They'd lose their job if they got slow.

S. Jayne Bradley

They had been told to thank God's grace
For there were those who'd take their place
As death and hunger followed near
Their lives and homes were stained with fear

This man of sixty never wept
He never dreamed while aching, slept
Each day he knew was on the wire
And so, he curbed, thoughts, wants, desire.

The union came in suit and tie
Hair so slick it would not dry,
His words were smooth like softest silk
The boss had warned them of his ilk

And there were those who'd never join
Even at the thought of coin
The Union man was not deterred
He knew what stakes his job inferred

Union cards would stoke the fires
He gave them out with union flyers.
The man whose words were always sweet
Came to them on worker's feet

A card was pressed in Bill's cracked palm
Not for him, a source of calm
But those that signed their life to dues
Would only see that war ensues.

Bill for now would hold his tongue
He knew his strength, but was not young
He watched the Bossman's sharpened whip
And felt it crack across his lip

Clocks Locks Corpses!

When others took the chance to fight
And spoke of change in dark of night
Bill, he thought, and thought with care
About the folks no longer there

Those that chose to speak their mind
And those who had been left behind
The union man now held his ire
Fuelled the forge and stoked the fire,

Bill found that he could sign his card
All his life he'd worked so hard
And now he wanted more than life
He raised his fist and dropped his knife

Work would slow and then would cease
No owner would be given peace
Hands untied would strike the few
The locks on chains they would undo

But after days of standing strong
Showing strength, with words and song
The winds had changed and not for good
And now ol' Bill, he understood

Truncheons hard, and heavy still
In hands who planned to maim and kill
Bill took beatings flesh and bone
But never took them on his own

He bled for friends and foes alike
The Union man still calling strike
As purses pinched began to rend
The Bossman's bosses began to bend

S. Jayne Bradley

Behind closed doors more words were said
Gaining ground for those who bled
A deal was struck and contracts signed
No worker would be left behind

A chorus rang as word got out
The Union man he gave a shout
For every man who worked the line
The future had begun to shine

The whistle blew, Bill took his post
And thought of those he loved the most
His heart would beat another shift
A heart of song his soul would lift

A lesser man would surely shrink,
But given time enough to think
Thoughts will drive one action sure
If we all fight, we'll all endure.

Pray for May

A line was stepped, a promise kept
Until the missionary wept
Three bells rang, the jailbirds sang
The air had such a vicious tang

And old May stood, within her hood
She was demure as so she should
There had been blood and swipes of mud
Her lawyer, he had been a dud

The gallows swung, old May had hung
If only she had held her tongue
So, in this age, the world's a stage
You'll need to want to turn the page

Her name was May, her hair was grey
And she had nowhere else to stay
Her skills were few, her brother knew
There was a thing that he could do

He welcomed May, she would not pay
Despite his wife still holding sway
The house was cold, and May was old
But she would do what she was told,

S. Jayne Bradley

Her brother's wife, had caused her strife
Was bent on fucking up her life
The chores were rough, the wife was tough,
And no task seemed to be enough

Her brother cared but never dared
To give what he and his wife shared
So May would grin, and lift her chin
She knew there was no way to win

There came a day, when poor old May
Had not arrived at church to pray
The pastor sees, no bended knees
And went to look just as you please

Upon his horse, quite high of course
To share his own brand of remorse
For no one skipped, his godly script
Or with his voice they would be whipped.

When he got there, he said a prayer
For there was blood most everywhere
It all felt wrong, and wasn't long
Before the sight had drawn the throng

All eyes had seen, and folks were keen
To know what caused this awful scene
The brother's wife's guts held the knife
No longer had she signs of life

But who held guilt, for blood was spilt
And left the blade up to the hilt
Who is to blame, what is their name
Who would own up to this shame?

Clocks Locks Corpses!

The brother said, his wife was dead
It was not he who made blood shed
There was a lie, within his eye
For that, he did not want to die

He told them May was there that day
Despite the fact she was away
Though May was out, there was a shout
To put her innocence in doubt

A search began, and while they ran
The shit had really hit the fan
The seeds were sown, and they were grown
The brother let May fight alone

They had found May, within a day
Her sullen face in shades of grey
She'd not been home, went out to roam
Expected back when moon would gloam

But she was dragged, and flogged and bagged
The killer they had thought they'd snagged
And then with dread, Old May had said
She didn't want the woman dead

Her alibi, she would not lie
But others paved the path to die
Her lawyer came, and made his name
Refuting each and every claim

But time was short, and out of court
He'd built his case they could not thwart
But on the stand, and by his hand
Things did not go like he had planned

S. Jayne Bradley

His voice was weak, his posture meek,
The outcome was now looking bleak
The magistrate had come in late
His character up for debate

The brother lied, the Pastor cried
And May's own words were tossed aside
As every word, the jury heard
Made honesty and truth absurd

The brother's ruse, soon hit the news
The court then filled with kangaroos
The other side, had nought to hide
The brother's words were never tried

A woman stained, and nothing gained
She would spend her last days chained
Though May was clean, she was now seen
And marred by people being mean

Old May had wept, no secrets kept
And word went out with whom she'd slept
Upon the street, and on her feet,
She'd done some things to make ends meet

She'd paid the cost, and all hope lost
Her defence had been lightly tossed
The brother's wife had caused her strife
And it was proved May took her life

The court adjourned, her stomach churned
She was no witch but would be burned
A curse was laid, debts to be paid
Her brother's soul would soon be weighed

Clocks Locks Corpses!

And as she stood on plank and wood
Around her head a noose and hood
In simple verse, she laid a curse
For those who lied would end up worse

Upon your soul, as black as coal
And as the night winds start to roll
As you accuse, your death ensues,
The Devil will collect his dues

And as she fell, no soul could tell
That May would not end up in hell
The silence came, and in their shame
Their souls were offered to the flame

A story's told, in days of old
When the night is getting cold
Of good old May, who hung that day
Who warned the town that they would pay

Time would tell and if the spell
Would conjure up the gates of hell
Perhaps they'll see, what was to be
If they had just set poor May free

Wolf and Rose

Chapter 1

A story once told by whispers in trees
That ripples and rustles in a cool winter's breeze
A story and song which no-one now knows
A tale of wolves and a woman named Rose

It was at a young age her mother had died
The illness came swift with the midmorning tide
It washed her away and with her the sun
The cruel hands of her father's she couldn't outrun

His reach had extended, and his hands were so strong
And in his tight grip she wouldn't last long
She didn't want much, but could not escape
Sooner or later, she'd succumb to this ape

She never expected that things could get worse
And Rose soon believed she was under a curse
For her father had gambled away all his gold
And to pay off his debts, his daughter he'd sold

After great many tears, and blows from his hand
Poor Rose had no strength on which she could stand
The deal had been struck and she had retreated

Clocks Locks Corpses!

Her father once more had left her defeated

The man she must wed was three times her age
And often flew off in a bloody red rage
He was rather rich but empty within
His eyes told her stories of debauches and sin

In her weakness and terror she wanted to hide
There was not a soul to whom she'd confide
Her father was law, and her wedding was soon
In all her despair she looked at the moon

So full and so round and brilliantly white
It shone in her room and cast out the night
Her fear was now gone, and her heart filled with hope
She went to her closet and pulled out a rope

Down to the street and then out of the town
Rose showed no sign she would ever slow down
She entered the trees with the moon as her guide
For deep in the woods, her time she would bide

The forest was thick, the shadows her shroud
Until the great moon went behind a dark cloud
She was dropped into pitch and her dress she had ripped
When over a root of a tree she had tripped

She continued on forward, her heart beating hard
In her mind she now knew she must be on guard
For there were more dangers in here than she thought
And worst of all was herself getting caught

Soon she took refuge by a black stagnant pool
She'd not drink its waters, she wasn't a fool
But there in the dark not far from her place

S. Jayne Bradley

There were two yellow eyes in a great wolfish face

Chapter 2

The world was in shadow behind these bright eyes
Memories now lost to the stars in the skies
A murmur of wind carries scents to his nose
Of wood smoke, and cherries, the softness of Rose

Attuned to the night, the moon shines so bright
And hungry for hunting and fresh blood tonight
His paws on the ground, they won't make a sound
And no soul will know of the terrible hound

Thunderous growl it roars from its chest
Shaking some birds from out of their nest
The crunching of bones, the hot blood and flesh
Oh, death tastes much better when the victim is fresh

He'd not had his fill from the small feathered treat
He hungered for more of the fresh tender meat
With blood on his lips and the hunt on his mind
He loped off to see what else he could find

The moon led him far from his usual grounds
He was partially led by unusual sounds
Two legged footsteps not far from his track
A feminine cry as the moon had turned black

With the speed of the wind in an unearthly pace
He followed the sound and started the chase
A far grander meal awaited his paws
A new kind of soul would find death in his jaws

Clocks Locks Corpses!

But there by the pond adorned all in white
A woman, a spirit invaded his sight
She was shining and glowing with long auburn hair
His hunger abated and his memories were there

Of rooftops and banquets and bright roaring fires
Of women, of music and human desires
They filled up his mind and pushed back the trees
The woodlands and creatures had vanished with ease

She looked at him deeply with saddened blue eyes
And she wasn't afraid, despite his large size
He paused by the pond, but he would not drink
For there in his thoughts he had started to sink

She gave him a smile and lifted a hand
He wouldn't move closer, so she moved to stand
Edging much nearer than he'd ever have dared
For not once in his life had he been this scared

A connection between them was beginning to grow
For reasons they knew they never would know
Her hand was so smooth upon his rough fur
There was nothing else in the world save for her

Then out of the dark came a man with a blade
He had followed the girl through the woods to the glade
He grasped her hand and went into the night
Taking the thing that made his world bright

Chapter 3

Not of death or of pain did Rose ever fear
The moment just called for her to be near
There was something about those honey gold eyes

S. Jayne Bradley

That made all her dreams, and her hopes start to rise

Blacker than midnight and blacker than ink
The wolf did not move, not even a blink
She knew she must touch him to make him be real
It was all that she wanted, to know him, to feel

It seemed like forever, and out of reach still
With just a small snap, he could strike out and kill
But Rose moved on closer, and the wolf did not move
Perhaps she thought dully, she had something to prove

As her fingers touched fur, she felt something new
The foundations for worry began to fall through
Her father and wedding for a moment forgotten
The walls of her prison were falling down rotten

And there in the dark with the beast of the night
She'd found all the courage she needed to fight
To return would be folly and foolish at best
And finally safe and warm she could rest

His great wolfish eyes would not leave her own
Together they knew they'd not be alone
And the wilds were there for them to explore
Through the woods to the fields to the glistening shore

But out of the darkness with a sword in his fist
Through the trees he had come and grabbed at her wrist
A mountainous man with eyes of cold ice
Her father had come so she must pay the price

Clocks Locks Corpses!

His fingers dug deep and scratched at her skin
This wasn't a battle she thought she could win
The fire he carried it burned with his hate
For the daughter worth less than the food on his plate

He cursed and he swore, and he wanted her dead
He wished that his wife had a boy child instead
No greater sin that his daughter had done
Was the day of her birth that she'd not been his son.

She stared at the woods as they left it behind
Her worries and pains returned so unkind
The safety of trees and the touch of the wild
Had rattled the bones and the heart of this child

Behind lock and key and the windows now barred
The beating he promised would leave her so scarred
A virtuous man whose promise he kept
So bloodied and beaten poor Rose, how she wept

For as she lay pained, with now broken dreams
Her hopes fell away to wedding dress seams
No forests or wolves to whisk her away
There in her torment he forced her to stay

Chapter 4

As the white dress had vanished deep into the black
The wolf had then wished that she would come back
It was the first thing he'd wished for in years
To his big yellow eyes had sprung many tears

For the day was now breaking the sun would now rise
Taking the thought and will from his eyes
But the morning was young and carried new light

S. Jayne Bradley

The gold and red dawn was ever so bright

As the sun now ascended and bringing the day
The memories of night would not fade away
He remembered the girl and thoughts that returned
And inside his mind they glittered and burned

Music now played and sang songs in his ears
The sweet taste of bread, mulled wine and beers
The glory of dancing and sleeping on silk
Of cooked meals and spices and gallons of milk

The road to his town was now on his mind
It was all rushing back, so long he'd been blind
Without second thoughts he followed the trail
To find the dear girl who had lifted his veil.

His hunting for food would soon be the past
He'd sleep in soft linen, eat fresh bread at last
Wear tailored suits and dance with his bride
His deep love for her would never subside

A sign soon appeared, and its markings were read
A skill he once thought he had lost from his head
The name brought back memories of things he had lost
A price he once paid, but forgotten the cost

His four-legged gait held control of his pace
And still he remained with wolf eyes and face
Soon he saw people in their normal routine
But they looked at this creature as something unclean

Sneers and sharp sticks, and screams filled with fear
Many had run when he wandered too near
With his head hanging low in a foul-smelling gutter
He hid from their blades and the curses they'd utter

Though this was his home, it wasn't the same
Whatever he knew, he'd forgotten his name
No claim on this place could a beast now take hold
No linen, no bread, and no shining gold

A kick to his ribs from a man dressed in grey
He drew out his sword, a wolf he would slay
But the wolf dodged the blow for he was too fast
And scarpered away this would not be the last

But as he left town, a sign caught his eye
The face of his love that he could not deny
Proclamations of union of her to a man
This turn of events went against his own plan.

Chapter 5

Late in the morning Rose lay on her bed
Her prospects left her despairing with dread
Caged in her room, with no way to be free
Her father had locked her in with his key

Soon the door opened, and he filled up its frame
With bile and with hatred he shouted her name
She looked back at him, with tears on her cheek
Her anger at him grew as he started to speak

He promised her pain if she ran off once more
That she would not rise from her bed anymore
With her as a price his debts were now clear

S. Jayne Bradley

And if she was lucky, she'd be dead in a year

His sallow face gleamed with the freedoms attained
Having a daughter had made him feel chained
And how he was passing his chains off to her
In place of the woods and the blackest of fur

The rights of the daughter are counted as few
And Rose had to pay all the debts that were due
Her soul was worth nothing to those in her life
And soon would be less as this other man's wife

She stared back in silence at her father's foul grin
Another man filled with darkness and sin
His words were her law, she had to obey
She would marry the man the very next day

He left her alone and locked her back in
Resigned and unable now Rose couldn't win
There were no more words or wolf by the pool
The illusion of freedom was under his rule

She lay on her bed and started to weep
The tears kept on falling 'til she fell asleep
And all that was wrong had soon passed behind
The chains fell away and the ropes that would bind

She dreamed of the forest, the marshes, and trees
The sound of the wind and the buzzing of bees
The flowers smelled sweet and coated with dew
She'd forgotten her room and all that she knew

She came to the pond which was clearer than glass
She walked to the shore and lay on the grass
The air was so sweet and at last she was free
The soft gentle wind had filled her with glee

And then he was there like the night just before
The yellow eyed wolf had sat by the shore
His fur it was gleaming a deep charcoal black
But it was a dream and she had to go back

Her hands touched him briefly and she saw a young boy
A lordly young soul with a sword as a toy
A curse laid upon him by magics unknown
Had then cast him down from a cold iron throne

Chapter 6

With deep seeded memories that burned to break free
The wolf he raced through each bush and each tree
The mark of the night was fresh in his skin
Memories and burdens had started to spin

His paws found their footholds in places untraced
Even in moonlight he'd not be outpaced
The forest held secrets and still would not speak
And he could find answers if he'd known what to seek

The smells on the air were clearer than day
Like colours, like birdsong, there was nothing grey
Her trail was like magic, so bright and so pure
Perhaps to his curse she could be the cure

And words he remembered he spoke with such ire
A promise was broken and thrown in the fire
No face had been shown as this memory past

S. Jayne Bradley

It flickered like candles, and it did not last

He quickened his pace and reached the woods end
Where city and forest had started to blend
And there up above like a princess on high
He lowered his head and let out a sigh

The towns tiny houses they filled him with dread
He longed for the shelter of tall trees instead
But fear was behind him, and far back it went
For this dear sweet angel had been heaven sent

He leaped to her window, with just her in mind
Leaving his reason and safety behind
She did not recoil, instead she reached out
She was a Goddess and he was devout

Her scent was of flowers and freshly tilled soil
Perhaps there was mint, and then primrose oil
Her eyes had been soft, and gentle her touch
It wasn't enough but it meant oh so much

The spell was soon broken by movement below
He knew in his heart it was time to go
He then tumbled down right onto to the street
And then he was off on his four wolfish feet

The big man gave chase, but the wolf was too quick
He easily dodged when the man threw a brick
Out of the town and into the trees
The wolf had escaped and did so with ease

There was much more that he had to learn
Of words and anger and fires to burn
A past made of sorrow that was buried down deep
But for now he was tired and he had to sleep

As old dreams encroached, he was slowing his pace
As he walked down old roads his paws left no trace
But torment and sadness was what now awaited
The smallest of hopes had now been negated

Chapter 7

That night when the dark had clutched at her heart
A howl at the moon it gave her a start
She ran to the window now blocked by the bars
But she still could see the moon and the stars

Where darkness there was she still found the light
And she had dared hope to see wolf eyes that night
She gripped at the bars and stood on her toes
She looked to the woods to where the path goes

Loping in black she caught the wolf's stride
He walked down the path not trying to hide
She reached out her hand as far as she could
But she couldn't reach to where the wolf stood

He howled once again his nose to the air
And all she could do was stand there and stare
Her heart it was racing, her eyes brimmed with tears
The wolf would do nothing to quiet her fears

And just when she thought her heart would have broken
She took a deep breath and these words she had spoken
"I feel that your name is there in my head

Some dream or some memory that I had left dead,"

The wolf cocked his head confused by her tone
She had tried to tell him he wasn't alone
For a moment it looked like he would just go
Perhaps he'd return but she did not know

In a leap and a bound he was on the ledge
His feet they had scrambled and clawed at the edge
The bars they had stopped him from getting to her
And she could just reach the ends of his fur

He bit at the bars and scratched at the wood
Making more noise than she thought he should
Her fingers they touched the top of his head
She prayed to her Gods that she'd not be wed

Far down below her father had stirred
Her wolfish companion would not be deterred
The ledge it gave way, he fell to the ground
A crash and a thump a terrible sound

He got to his feet and looked up once more
Just as her father burst out the front door
With a shout and bellow he gave the wolf chase
And Rose ducked right down to conceal her face

Her father returned with his face red with rage
His journey upstairs it would take an age
But as she awaited the blows that would come
Her heart it was beating so fast in a thrum

He'd come back for her, in her darkest hour
With magical speed he'd come to her bower
If love could be real, she'd call out his name
This monstrous wolf she knew she could tame

Chapter 8

The words and their meanings had started to fade
And so had his thoughts of the girl in the glade
He felt a strong hunger deep down in his gut
And was once again just a blood thirsty mutt

But now it was different, it wasn't the same
Somewhere deep down he had carried a name
In memories now dust and faded with age
In lines now unwritten in ink on a page

His thoughts they now rumbled and soon would return
A flame deep inside him would flicker and burn
The magic was breaking and this he knew well
No Wizard on earth casts a permanent spell

But still as he saw that her face was the sign
Out from his throat came a howl and whine
No mortal on earth would stop him this day
He would love his girl, and someone would pay

He slathered and snarled, his world crashing down
He'd had his fill of this horrible town
Tired and hungry but not yet too spent
He ran through the woods to pick up her scent

The sun dappled through and made the earth shine
He knew in his heart that things would be fine

S. Jayne Bradley

His spirit was strong and he had the will
And only for her he was sure he could kill

The glade and the pool he found as they were
A few moments later the scent, it was her
A delicate trail that weaved through the trees
Had almost been lost in the cold winter's breeze

It filled him with love and the strength he would need
Growing within like the tiniest seed
A forest of will would grow in his chest
Until he found her, he could never rest

So many nights at the moon he had bayed
Until some old debt he had to have paid
But memories were gone and wolf he remained
Leaving him lost, his humanity drained

And then came the girl, a delicate flower
Had entered the woods at an ungodly hour
He followed her path over root, over streams
He must go and save her, the girl of his dreams

The wedding bells chimed as her home was in sight
He wasn't too late, things would happen right
And as he drew up to her humble abode
A carriage sped off quite fast down the road

Her scent it was strong, he could not let go
Went the carriage to church with a werewolf in tow
The smell of her grew the closer he got
And he had to give chase before he forgot

Chapter 9

The dress was embroidered with gold and with lace
And powder was smeared all over her face
Her lips and her cheeks were now blushing red
And to top it all off she wished she was dead

A servant girl came with ribbons and string
And then tried to soothe her by starting to sing
Her voice remained gentle, lilting, demure
She sang of how love was so magic and pure

She sang of sweet flowers to gather in spring
And how the kind groom would give her a ring
Golden and glowing encrusted with gems
And thousands of roses with long uncut stems

That everyone waited for the pretty young bride
There was no need for tears and no need to hide
That love found a way of working things through
And there was not much that poor Rose could do

A mirror was pulled from under a sheet
The bride was dragged up from out of her seat
She saw her reflection as if in a dream
And frozen in place she started to scream

The servant girl hushed her and silenced her voice
For this was her wedding and Rose had no choice
So with a harsh grip she took her outside
And then to the church in a carriage she'd ride

Fixed in her spot by the servant girl's grip
With the sound of the horses and a terrible whip
It cracked and it sang, and she knew how it feels

To have human devils so close on your heels

From inside the carriage Rose peered at the street
Wishing that she could soon make a retreat
Time was now short, she wanted to run
To fall into pieces and leave it undone

Her strength lay in hope her wolf would appear
Tear apart strangers and show them real fear
Her eyes closing tightly to wish this a dream
Feeling all twisted and wanting to scream

Blank staring faces they watched her pass by
Not knowing if able, she would choose to die
The clouds they now lingered as if to perceive
What Gods she would call on if she could believe

The carriage drew closer to her story'sies end
A church full of people, not one was a friend
A steeple and church bells that rang in the day
Calling for good folks to come in and pray

She could only watch as they rolled up outside
Though she was dragged out, she stood there with pride
She'd not make a scene nor ask to be free
And go to her fate with her dignity

Chapter 10

The carriage had rolled at a terrible pace
As if they were now winning the horrible race
For people had seen him and slowed him right down
All of the folk in this one-horse town

Clocks Locks Corpses!

They threw rocks at his body and laughed as he fell
Each blow coincided with the ringing church bell
They chased him off course and cursed and they swore
But he was no wolf, no not anymore

He started to feel the spell fall apart
With each heated breath and beat of his heart
Though he looked like a wolf, he felt like a man
He felt the beast slipping the faster he ran

The carriage turned corners and was far out of view
The scent was his guide as he chased it through
He knew the town well in the back of his mind
Without the fine carriage, the church he could find

Through gutters and basements and rooms full of food
The shouting and stones wouldn't dampen his mood
He knew the right way through the memory and scent
The carriage was lost, didn't know where it went

In through a butcher's and then through a store
Stealing a snack then back out the door
With hunger at bay his strength now his best
Feeling love rise with the hope in his chest

And there was the church at the end of the street
Soon he could rest his world weary feet
How long he'd been lost he was sure no one knows
But nothing else mattered but his dear sweetest Rose

As he approached, it all flooded back
The reason for wolves and fur turning black
For one small mistake had cost him his crown
And left him to watch his kingdom fall down

A promise once made for him by another
A proposal was made by his own dear old mother
His bride to be was a devious witch
Her heart had been black as boiling hot pitch

Afraid and ashamed of his parents' bad choice
He decided to run and it cost him his voice
And the spell that was cast had come from his bride
When he had left, he had chosen to hide

Hurt and betrayed, the woman had left
A mother's dead son was simply a theft
The once bride had vowed if a wolf had a heart
The spell would then crack and soon fall apart

Rose was his saviour, his glorious queen
What a fool and a beast, he had been so mean
But all would resolve, and he'd save her from this
A monstrous form of marital bliss

Chapter 11

She would soon be tied to a man with no care
Who hated and beat her and was always unfair
But Rose knew her duty and she knew it well
Now she was doomed with the sound of a bell

It hung in the air and rang in her head
Caused musings of woe and feelings of dread
The church was in view, her father in wait
His dark massive frame was there by the gate

Clocks Locks Corpses!

He glowered and leered with a sick twisted smile
This told her that he had been there a while
He was dressed rather well but didn't look fine
The clothes did not fit, and he smelled of cheap wine

The servant girl's grasp was loose for the trade
She passed over Rose and then she was paid
Her father had grinned, his fingers held fast
He would not let go as he'd done in the past

The church was quite lovely, small and so sweet
Beneath some tall trees at the end of the street
The front door was open, so tall and so wide
Her father gripped tighter and led her inside

Her veil was now low and hid her bruised face
She'd soon walk on in and then take her place
To take up her role beside her new man
For then she would die, and that was her plan
❦

Her eyes searched the streets, but no-one had come
She lowered her head and felt very dumb
For what would a wolf know of love and desire
It only knows trees, the pond and the briar

No promise was made, there was no rule broken
He'd not had a ring, a gift, or a token
They just had the moon and the stars in the skies
And she had been lost in his great yellow eyes

The doors stood before her a threshold to cross
To live or to die it wasn't her loss
Hope had now drained her and left her a hole
Right in the place where she'd carried her soul

The doors loomed above her, so tall and so great
And through them she'd walk and then meet her fate
All whimsy and magic would be left outside
Her future uncertain her dreams now denied

The sound of the bells had felt like her doom
As she had been led into a side room
Her make up was fixed, her hair tidied up
She was offered wine in a small wooden cup

Then she was led straight into the aisle
Her hope had been lost, there was no denial
Her footsteps were light and slow to begin
She blinked away tears and forced out a grin

Chapter 12

He knew there was fire and curse on her breath
Something forgotten was reeking of death
Yellow blonde hair with ribbons and bows
The feeling of dread and horror it grows

Marking the days and shadows grow long
This feeling of evil it grows very strong
Of teacups and lace and canapés too
Something once borrowed and then something blue

The wolf now remembered another such place
Before he had paws and strange wolfish face
A prince he'd once been with a promise to keep
His parents had loved him, but their price was too steep

Clocks Locks Corpses!

While pretty enough, his bride was quite cold
Like pieces of meat, she'd been bought and sold
But he tried to love her, as best that he could
Despite that her heart was made out of wood

She forced her desire, and wanted his gold
He was quite young, his parents were old
She told him no secrets and told him no lies
And he didn't care for her devilish eyes

A woman of stone, of ice, and of steel
She carried no love, had no heart to feel
It came to a head on the day they'd be wed
And he had decided he'd rather be dead

But still he had waited 'til she said I do
Then he revealed that he was now through
The crowd they had gasped and then they all jeered
It ended much worse than he'd ever feared

And he walked away, to her turned his back
Then she cast spells, and that magic was black
With a small muted whisper he started to change
His body had turned into something strange

And she had then told him that he'd not return
Until there was nothing for him left to burn
The church was engulfed with magical flame
She'd taken his family, and stolen his name

Then out of the town as a wolf he had fled
Noting on which trails and paths he had tread
He counted the stars 'til their names were lost
And many cold mornings were spent in the frost

He awoke with gasp his heart now aflame
Buried down deep he had found his name
A price would be paid, to set his Rose free
This promise he'd keep for it was the key

Footprints in mud and drool in his jaws
Tracking her scent with his nose and his paws
The church loomed ahead so pure and so white
And this wolf before it, he wanted a fight

Chapter 13

The music was sweet and caused her much pain
The tears from her eyes were falling like rain
The handful of folks who sat in the pews
Believed tears of joy were such happy news

At the end of the aisle stood the man to be groom
And he had the blackest heart in the room
Ancient and grey and a few years from death
He seemed just three seconds from his very last breath

Old rotten teeth were set loose in his face
Of any good humour there was not a trace
He leered and he hissed and licked at his lip
The drool from his mouth was starting to drip

The priest at the front, he paid them no mind
He just had a face that appeared to be kind
Rose focused on him and no other thing
And not on her father who brought out the ring

Clocks Locks Corpses!

She felt so apart, so distant from all
And she felt so tiny, and they all seemed so tall
Helpless, despairing, she continued her pace
And thousands of tears still poured down her face

From one hand to next she was passed on like gold
And even wrapped warm, she still felt so cold
For in such a place where there is no love
No union is blessed from God up above

Her hands were now taken in craggy old claws
Instead of the softness of dark wolfish paws
His dark sunken eyes were filling with lust
Her life in his hands she could never trust

The music kept playing to the sound of his words
She was sure that in here her prayers would be heard
The priest said his lines, so well they were learned
His place in the church was something he earned

But his words sounded bitter to Rose's kind ear
For maybe he knew of her sadness and fear
And from where he stood, just as helpless as she
It was not the right time to try and break free

The music soon stopped, and the silence was worse
Out came the ring, her chains, and her curse
The priest said her name and asked her to speak
But she couldn't move, her heart was too weak

A blow from her father then opened her eyes
She spoke out her words, but they sounded like lies
A sigh of relief had come from the crowd
As her new husband said his own part aloud

Rose was now lost in the sale of her life
The loss of her freedom had cut like a knife
Soon they would leave and go to his bed
Perhaps at this time she was better off dead

Chapter 14

He howled at the doors but could not be heard
But the wolf at the gates could not be deterred
His strength it was growing like a tempest within
He clawed at the door, these men would not win

Slivers of wood now fell on stone stairs
As well as a handful of little black hairs
But of no concern this was in his view
The door was too thick, and he had to break through

No more would he wait for answers to come
To all but his Rose he was cut off and numb
The scrape of his paws on the handles and frame
Called up more memories, the last thing, his name

For thick in the past, it was buried down deep
And out of the dark it started to creep
Then when he found Rose, and could not recall
He started to think he had no name at all

They fell into place, each piece of his past
His name then came forward, his true name at last
To some it seemed simple, too simple to lose
But it's easy to lose things that you never use

Clocks Locks Corpses!

The door would not open for him to save Rose
But the scent of her beauty assaulted his nose
He beat at the door and howled to the sky
If he could not have her then he'd choose to die

The door then fell through with a thunderous crack
And there was his Rose who was now looking back
The guests echoed back in horrified screams
And she in his eyes was just like his dreams

Alive, in his eyes, a strengthening flame
All he desired was to just say her name
For the name he now held so tight in his hand
Had fit well with his and they sounded so grand

The men drew their swords on the beast by the door
Hoping its blood would be shed on the floor
The wolf snarled and snapped and started to grow
His howls started deeply and rose up so slow

He saw his Rose beaming, and warmed at her smile
He hadn't felt joy like this in a while
The men with their blades began to draw near
But he was a wolf and a man with no fear

He did not attack but awaited their strike
These two men weren't strong and were so much alike
Wicked and weak and hungry with greed
But nothing would slake their thirst or their need

He'd kill them so quick with gnashing of jaws
Unless they would flee and give him no cause
But it looked like they wanted him dead at their feet
For the sale of his fur and the taste of wolf meat

Chapter 15

As the church door crashed down, she let out a scream
And in through the door had lurched like a dream
Her wolf, he had come to her rescue at last
But the distance between them was still very vast

She wanted to run but was now more afraid
Her father enraged, had pulled out his blade
The fight would soon start, and blood would be shed
One of them would now find themselves dead

Despite all he'd done, all the pain that he gave
She did not desire to dig a mass grave
The other guests fled for fear of their end
Now she was alone with her wolf to defend

Somewhere she'd found her deep inner fire
With small silent prayers she built it up higher
With his great yellow eyes, she fed the hot flames
For she was his Rose, and she dreamed he was James

The strength of his will to break down the door
Had flowed into her, not afraid anymore
She walked down the step to approach the three foes
To face all her problems, her troubles, and woes

It was a bright day, through the door she could see
And outside was the place that she could be free
She stepped past the groom and pushed back his blade
And whispered, "The debt will never be paid,"

Clocks Locks Corpses!

The groom he stepped back, his blade he put down
She watched his strength ebb, he started to frown
No more did he speak of love and devotion
To evil it is a painful emotion

Her father still keen to start up a fight
Had circled the wolf and closed in so tight
His blade was quite sharp and ever so clean
That you couldn't tell what fights it had seen

Both man and beast had teeth that were bared
And neither of them would be running off scared
But Rose knew them well and knew what to say
For this was much more than her wedding day

The gentlest touch she placed on his arm
This monstrous man would do no more harm
Still full from the pain of the loss of his wife
That it would hurt for the rest of his life

Rose understood but she could not forgive
For under his thumb was no way to live
He turned to her with such fear in his eyes
Gone was the hatred and the mountain of lies

Her touch fell away and so did his hold
And in this soft moment he seemed to grow old
Rose then stepped back and said not a word
For all of her thoughts she was sure he had heard

Chapter 16

The pain he was feeling had spread to each limb
His vision and senses were growing so dim
He felt he was changing and returning to form
And inside his flesh was a gathering storm

At first fur was falling and standing on end
The scratches and bruises were beginning to mend
As he faced off his foe to rescue his Rose
He felt his skin tighten and shorten his nose

With each passing breath the wolf would soon fade
His debt that was owed now humbly paid
But the fight was not over, for someone must win
And then his new life would gladly begin

The man was much stronger, and he had the will
He had been a man who loved a good kill
He snarled and he snapped with teeth that were blunt
The worst kind of teeth when out on the hunt

The change was so smooth but carried much pain
He'd face the discomfort, there was much to gain
A swipe of the blade and a swish of his tail
The monstrous man was starting to pale

For he was now watching the wolf fall away
The father cried "Demon!" and started to pray
Then she had come like a spirit or ghost
And she was the girl he would love the most

Clocks Locks Corpses!

Like an Angel she came all dressed up in white
Glowing and shining with unearthly light
Her smile was wide, and sweet and serene
And he could believe that she was a queen

A glorious maiden whose strength would not end
Who breaks ancient spells and old pains would mend
For her father had seen what she had become
In silence he stared, he had been struck dumb

As the last of the beast had fallen away
Rose's old man had no cause to stay
He'd lost what he had and lost what he owed
All he had reaped was what he had sowed

The fur was bare skin, the hair was still black
But no longer grew all over his back
On two legs he stood so tall and so proud
And now he could speak all his secrets out loud

But nothing was said, for they only stared
For this moment was theirs and they hadn't dared
He opened his arms and searched in her face
He wanted no more than her tender embrace

The time it grew longer as she ran to his side
The warmth had returned with the mid-morning tide
Her wolf or her man she didn't much care
He loved her, he saved her, and he was still there

Chapter 17

Together at last and forever entwined
A spell of the ages together would bind
She stared in his eyes, still burnished with gold
And she loved him more for the story they told

He then looked at her, his angel in white
Who broke the black spell in the forest that night
She loved him from then, and with him she'd go
And why she chose him, they both would not know

They both had been trapped and each other to save
To find their own strength and learn to be brave
For what they both wanted they would have to fight
But they had believed it would be all right

Now she was there, and he was there too
There was a small question of what they would do
His throne was long gone, and she had no home
Where would they wander, and where would they roam

But fear of the future seemed so far away
The sun was so bright on this wonderful day
So, finding a robe for the wolf man to wear
They left the small church without thought, without care

The wind brought the scent of fresh baking bread
A wonderful thought had then filled his head
But he looked as angel, his dearest sweet Rose,
And down on one knee he had to propose

Clocks Locks Corpses!

As she said yes, the wind picked up speed
Something was wrong, yes quite wrong indeed
A pain they both felt deep down in their bones
And out of their mouth they uttered their moans

She felt her dress split and his robe hit the floor
He wasn't a man, no not anymore
But she too was changing her hands turned to claws
Instead of her teeth, she had fangs in her jaws

On the bright sunny day, a new spell was spun
The moment the first and been broken, undone
The promise of love had come with a price
For the debt of the woman, it must be paid twice

They shared their first kiss that would be their last
As they fell to the will of the spell that was cast
Forever as wolves but never alone
They both had their breath, their flesh and their bone

To the woods they both ran and passed through the trees
Together they smelled the scents on the breeze
Of woodsmoke and cherries and cool shallow streams
The wonderous woods were made of their dreams

No more were they human, the change was complete
They ran on four paws instead of two feet
And for all that they lost, they still had their names
A she-wolf called Rose and a wolfman called James

S. Jayne Bradley

Horse And Norm

The sun was low and spirits high,
No cloud obscured the bright blue sky
The trees would sway as summer chills,
Their whispers heard beneath the hills.

Horse and Norm were by the lake,
A long-held dream was theirs to take,
Their jolly boat still on the shore
And time, they knew they wanted more.

Their childhood wish had been acquired
And just before the two retired,
For many years they'd scrimped and saved
For what they both had always craved.

Their calls and shouts the forest heard
And scaring every kind of bird,
Their flapping wings dislodged the leaves
That floated down on summer's breeze.

A bond had been forged in water and flame
A friendship and past that carried no name

There was a splash, the boat was out
And Norm, he gave a gleeful shout.

Clocks Locks Corpses!

He waved to Horse still on the sand
And asked him if he'd like a hand,

But Horse, he stood with hands on knees
Breathing hard and with a wheeze
He raised a thumb, said all was good,
A few more tasks, then join he would.

Beside the road his Ute was parked
Within the lines so clearly marked.
The lake then drew his worried stare.
"I hope it's not too cold in there."

He then stepped out, his head held high,
The icy lake crawled up his thigh,
A mighty king from ancient halls
Until the water reached his balls.

Entwined in a dream had once been so bright
The passage of time would turn out the light

The day was spent with hooks and line,
Drinking beer and feeling fine.
Horse and Norm relived old days,
Of ocean shores in memory's haze.

Two quiet nights they'd planned to stay
Even if the sky turned grey
The catch was good and worth the wait,
They'd stay until they had no bait.

They counted fish, their haul admired,
The first star came, and they felt tired.
Horse went to lie upon his bed
His thoughts eclipsed with strangest dread.

Horse wasn't sure, but things were wrong,
And wondered if they'd stayed too long.
Into the night his dark thoughts spun
Until his sleepy brain was done.

The days that will follow are clearer than most
The vigilant man will not leave his post

When morning came, the lake was smooth
But Horse's thoughts, it could not soothe.
They baited hooks and cast their lines
As wind picked up between the pines.

Norm felt a fish tug at his rod.
He then gave Horse a knowing nod.
They reeled it in with skill and care
The fish they caught, it wasn't there.

The silver box was worn and old
The keyhole's where the hook took hold.
Horse stared long then laughed with glee,
"Drop your line and catch the key."

Norm pulled it in and held it tight
Fingers clutched with all his might.
The box unhooked and in his grasp
He tried to open up the clasp.

A courteous whisper before their demise
The shadows slip through as darkness will rise

The box it glinted and it gleamed
And it was more than what it seemed.
Patterned swirls of strange design

Clocks Locks Corpses!

And such detail in every line.

Horse then saw his best friend change
From something safe to something strange.
A certain look, the way he'd move
But in a way Horse couldn't prove.

Norm then turned to Horse and smiled.
His eyes were bright, a little wild.
"I'll open this when we return.
For now, it's none of our concern."

The Norm he knew was baiting hooks
But flicked the box strange hungry looks.
Something itched in Horse's brain.
He struggled with his thoughts again.

The fates had been waiting, for something to bind
On a dark shadowed shore, the stars had aligned

Overhead the clouds had rolled.
It started raining, light and cold.
The wind was blowing through the trees
And Horse and Norm were ill at ease.

Their bucket filled with many fish,
It showed that they'd fulfilled their wish.
A day's success then moved to night
As two men drank their Amstel light.

There was no talk, no memory lane,
And all attempts were made in vain
As Norman's gaze was getting mired
In the silver box desired.

S. Jayne Bradley

Horse's throat he tried to clear
And got up off his derriere.
"I think it's time we went to bed,
If I stay up, tomorrow's dead."

A horror had come from down in the deep
And into their hearts it had started to creep

Norm hummed and ha'ed with all his might.
He questioned if his friend was right.
With heavy feet Horse held his ground
And Norm stood up without a sound.

The boat was still, it didn't rock,
And all his thoughts he'd try to block
But something still scratched at his mind
And left all sane thoughts far behind.

The morning came and all was good
Felt better than Horse thought it should.
But questions could be held at bay
So they could fish another day.

It was near noon, the sun was high
And time to leave for somewhere dry.
They packed their boat and headed home
Before the light began to gloam.

All mountains crumble, are swallowed as stone
And earth will endure, outlast flesh and bone

When Horse parked up and let Norm out
He spoke his question in a shout.
"You'll tell me what you find in there?"
What Norm had said Horse could not hear.

Clocks Locks Corpses!

The nights were cold, a week passed by.
Horse heard no word, but had to try.
He called up Norm who answered quick,
His voice had sounded stuffed and thick.

"I've caught a cold," Norm said and frowned.
"I feel like I have gone and drowned,
I'm not quite sure I'll be okay.
The box was empty by the way."

Though not relieved, Horse wished him well
And offered to stop by a spell.
But Norm's response was cold and swift
And Horse had felt their friendship shift.

One man who is blinded by what he can't see
And there's nowhere to turn, and nowhere to flee

"You cannot help, I'm rather sick."
The phone cut off, an angry click
And Horse had felt his blood run cold,
But he'd not do as he was told.

He packed a lunch, a case of beers
And went to face his darkest fears.
A man like him won't leave his friend
He'd fight until the bitter end.

So off he drove to Norm's small house,
The one he shared with Jill, his spouse.
There was no sound, no windows cracked.
He called Norm's name, his nerves now wracked.

S. Jayne Bradley

For moments there was not a sound,
No sign of movement could be found.
The silence scared him more and more
But still he walked up to the door.

A lingering shadow writhes beneath mortal skin
And causing a rot and decay from within

He steeled himself and then he knocked
And tested if the door was locked.
He strained his ears and closed his eyes
And prepped his mind for this surprise.

The things he heard from deep within
Had set his guts to cycle spin.
It was no voice he'd recognise,
It sounded just like swarming flies.

The door it creaked and then it cracked.
Horse raised his hands as if attacked.
The face between the frame and door,
It was not Norm, not anymore.

His eyes were grey and sunken deep,
Seemed like he'd been short on sleep.
His skin was red and badly scratched,
It looked like from him bugs had hatched.

As fingers and nails run ragged on flesh
Blood spurts from old wounds now opened afresh

Horse recoiled, and caught his breath,
It stank like Norm had messed with death.
Horse stumbled back, his eyes went wide,
Could not find words if he had tried.

Clocks Locks Corpses!

Norm clutched the door so firm in place,
His body hid, showed half his face.
Out came his words bitter and broke.
What ghastly hell had Norm awoke?

Norm's three front teeth then tumbled out,
More boils before his eyes did sprout.
"Jill isn't well, does not look great,
I think I left things far too late."

Horse shook his head, looked to the street,
Finding strength to move his feet.
Norm reached a hand, said, "All is well."
But to his fear, three fingers fell.

What could be foreseen has now been obscured
No answer to prayers as the shadows endured

Tripping on cracks and chips in stone,
Ambulance called from mobile phone,
Into his Ute he struggled in vain
And dropped his keys into the drain.

Sirens were heard and Horse remained.
EMTs' eyes silently strained.
Covered up, completed tasks,
Disgust behind their fabric masks.

No one spoke as bodies taken,
Just a wave that left him shaken.
A broken heart, his friend now dead,
Horse had no time, no tears to shed.

S. Jayne Bradley

There was a task still incomplete,
And out of fear he might retreat,
The silver box he'd have to take
And cast it back into the lake.

Down to the dark where the light cannot touch
It seems like a lot, but it wasn't that much

Funerals came, the world was bleak,
Then off to Norm's one day that week.
What he had held, he could not bear
 Now that his friend would not be there.

When he went back, the house was cold,
The food was off and caked with mould.
What he had thought should be undone
If he had known, he would have run.

He went inside and looked around.
With great relief, the box was found.
The bagged-up box against his hip
And it would take its final trip.

Horse, in his Ute, looked to his left.
Norman was gone, he was bereft.
Behind, the boat was towed along
'Cause keeping it felt very wrong.

He soon arrived down at the lake
And felt like it was no mistake.
He placed the box on Norman's chair
And with it left his pain, despair.

Clocks Locks Corpses!

The flames rose high upon the deck.
He must be sure, he had to check.
It was a shock when jumping in,
The water cold on bones and skin.

Off the boat and onto the shore
He'd watch until there was no more.
The water kept the fire tamed,
The boat and box were now reclaimed.

Horse, he cried and wiped his eyes.
Stood on the wharf, flames on the rise.
And as night fell and cloaked the land
He felt an itch upon his hand.

S. Jayne Bradley

Acknowledgements

There are many people to thank. Firstly, thank you to Jennifer Garcia, for seeing the value in these stories.

Secondly my family. To my Mum and Dad for raising me right and supporting me in this process. To my sister Rachel, who is responsible for zhuzhing up my hatchet job of an attempt at cover art. (Don't tell her I said I think she is very talented). Then to my brother Matthew, who always believed in me and is always impressed with my work.

We're just under halfway through this, by the way.

Next up, to the NW, who were there at the beginning, when I started writing these things twelve to thirteen years ago, Sunny, Ashley, Brendan, Edan, Elly, Halie, Hannah, Rebekah, Vic, Alice and Paige thank you for your continued encouragement. Even though I've been so busy the last 4 years you all mean the world to me.

To my friend Dayna, if it wasn't for you pushing me to go to University, I would still be in Hamilton in the call centre. You are one of the best and bravest people I know.

Now to the North Shore Writers Group, who were there at the end of this book. Tim, Bruce, Elizabeth, Nikky, Sharron, Andrew, Christopher, Nicola, Jennifer, Frances, Alex, Sarah, and Mark. Your continued feedback and friendship is an important part of my life. I always look forward to our meetings, and I have learned so much from all of you.

To my DnD friends, Justin, Ash, Brodie, Kass, Bonnie, Jennifer (again), whose connections indirectly led to this moment. It's been a weird ass road.

Clocks Locks Corpses!

And also thank you to Melanie and Katrina, they get a special mention as my oldest and dearest friends.

Lastly, I would like to thank myself. Thank you for sticking it out longer than you planned or expected. This is like a prize at the end of a race. Yeah, it was a slog, but you made it, buddy. I'm proud of you.

About the Author

Ten years ago, Suzanne Jayne Bradley showed up at a friend's thirtieth birthday party dressed as a poet. Fortunately, the theme of the party was "What you wanted to be when you grew up" and no one who knows her was surprised by Suzanne's choice, because her love of writing and poetry is long-standing.

She has been crafting poems since primary school and at sixteen even won third place in a high school writing competition (for a little tiny poem of no consequence, but she's still proud of it!).

Now she's forty years old and has finally seen her dream come true with the publication of her anthology of fun, spooky poems, *Clocks Locks Corpses!* It is the result of a series of slightly unbelievable events involving Dungeons and Dragons, pizza, and a supportive writers' group. (You had to be there to understand.)

Over the years, Suzanne has worked various jobs, from cafés to call centres and even on film shoots. Currently, she lives in Auckland, New Zealand, working in an office for a manufacturing company while continuing to nurture her love of writing.

With her first book now published, she is committed to her new dream of writing poetry for a living. Finger's crossed!